The

War about

Forever

By Joe McCormick

George Douglas Matthews was a mathematics genius. He was the smartest person I have ever known. George had a very hard time mixing with people. He believed in God and the Lord Jesus Christ As his pastor I wanted so much for him to find his place in the Body of Christ. That day never came. George passed in August 2013 This Novel is dedicated to him.

Book cover by: *Real* Gallery   UFO Blonde Mountains

But the serpent said to the woman, "You will not surely die.
For God knows that when you eat of it your eyes will be opened,
And you will be like God, Gen 3:5 ESV

This is the original lie

And as people migrated from the east, they found a plain in the land of Shinar and settled there.

And they said to one another, "Come, let us make bricks, and burn them thoroughly." And they had brick for stone, and bitumen for mortar.

Then they said, "Come, let us build ourselves a city and a tower with its top in the heavens, and let us make a name for ourselves, lest we be dispersed over the face of the whole earth.
Gen 11: 2-4 ESV

This is the original religion

Prologue

The flood of the Ohio River in 1937 took place between January and February 1937. Damages stretched from Pittsburgh Pennsylvania to Cairo Illinois One million people were left homeless. 385 were dead and property damage reached $500 million ($8,723 billion when adjusted for inflation as of January 2019)
The river reached its peak on January 26th at 79.9 more than 25 feet higher than the flood stage in Madison Indiana. It was the highest level ever recorded. 9 feet above the previous record set in 1884.

Chapter 1

Douglas Eaton volunteered in the recovery effort to get the city of Madison Indiana and Jefferson county back on its feet. The first few days were spent making sure the citizens of Madison had a roof over their heads. Clean water to drink and hot food to eat. When the water was low enough to drive the streets, Doug volunteered to drive upriver toward Vevay Indiana, to check the citizens living on the river bank.

The folks in the first few cabins only needed clean water. They were doing well compared to the citizens of Madison, who were hit very hard by the flood. These folks were a different breed of people. They were roughed and very independent. Doug made a note that they needed water and drove his Ford roadster on up the river.

Next he turned into the pull-over at Rabbit Hill, where the Matthews family lived. When Doug stepped out of his Roadster, he looked up the steps leading up the steep river bank to the Matthews cabin. At the top of the steps, on the side deck, John Matthews sipped from his cup of coffee. "Are you okay, down there?" he yelled down to Doug. "How about yourself? Do you need any assistance?" he yelled back. "No! We're all fine. We don't need a thing!" John answered. "Do you have drinking water?" Doug asked. "Plenty" John assured him.

Before Doug climbed back into his car, John asked him "Are you hungry? There's no restaurants between here and Vevay" Doug's stomach was growling. "I won't be putting you out?" Doug yelled up at him. "Not at all! Maw always cooks too much for the youngsters" he answered. Doug understood, it would be an insult for him to refuse to eat with John and his family. He closed the car door and started up the long flight of steps to the cabin.

When he reached the top John had a fresh cup of coffee waiting for him. "Hope you like your coffee, black" he said handing the cup to Doug. "20 years in the Navy. That was the only way I could drink it" he answered John. "I served too in the big war" John told him "I was stationed on the BB37" he continued. "That was the Oklahoma, right?" Doug asked as he leaned on the deck rail next to John. "Did you know it?" John asked. I was on the AD2, the USS Melville, we pulled beside you guys in the Ireland. I had to see the new oil burning boiler. John smiled "I never went down in the hole, I was a deck-ape" he told Doug. "I was a Machinist Mate but I had my turns shoveling coal" Doug told him. "I had to see the Navy's the first oil-burner" he added.

"Come you get-it!" Mrs. Matthews yelled from inside the cabin. From the deck it sounded like a herd of elephants charged the dinner table. John yelled at his children to settle down at the table. "Georgie! Get over here!" he yelled once more at his oldest son who sat on the sofa studying a math problem. Georgie put his pad and pencil away and joined everyone waiting for him at the dinner table.

After John gave "Grace" he asked Georgie "what all his ciphering was about?" He answered his Father reluctantly "I was listening on the radio that the water level was 71.8 feet at 9:00 this morning and 70.3 feet at 11:00am two hours later. The river is 600 feet wide at the high water mark so I was figuring how many gallons of water flowed down river in those two hours" he answered his Father. "Georgie what is the good of knowing that?" John asked, rebuking him. "It's good for nothing. I just like to figure out stuff like that" he shamefully answered his Father. "He is so smart but he doesn't have any common sense" John complained to Doug.

Doug felt sad for Georgie because his Father didn't understand how gifted his son was. "How old is Georgie?" Doug asked John. "He'll turn 13 next week" he answered. "I imagine your Teacher at school, loves you" Doug said smiling. But the entire table erupted in laughter. "Georgie got kicked out of school" his younger Brother laughed. "The teachers at school are stupid!" Georgie yelled. "Enough of that!" John yelled at his sons.

"Georgie can't keep his mouth shut. He corrects his Teachers all the time" John explained. "But they were wrong, Dad! I proved it to them!" Georgie protested. "You should show respect for your Teachers" John corrected him. Georgie stopped eating his beans and cornbread and stared silently into the air. "He has to do his school work at home all by himself" John said. "He reads his text books and takes the tests. We turn them into the school where they give him a grade…He makes straight "A's" Georgie's Mother said with pride. "And he'll be graduating high school this year" she boosted.

Doug was shocked "but he not even 13 years old. How can he be graduating from high school?" he remarked. "I earned it from my grades" Georgie chimed in smiling from ear to ear. "But he still lacks common sense" his Father reminded him. "What's your favorite subject Georgie?" Doug asked him. "Math, I do Math the best" he answered Doug's question.

"We need some one at the court house who is good in Math" Doug said. "We need them to keep our record of expenses correct

for the government" he added. "Are you offering Georgie a job?" John asked. "We'll have to check his skills but if he's as good as you say, we could sure use his skills" Doug said. "I won't allow him to work for free" John remarked. "If he can do the job, he will get a check" Doug said.
"My old Ford is broke down and I can't get it fixed, I can't get him to the courthouse" John said. "I come and get him until he can get your car going with his first pay check" Doug said. "Then he can go to work as soon as possible" John told him. "I'll pick him up at 7:00 am. Down on the pull-over" Doug said.

When the meal was finished, Doug thanked the Manter family for their hospitality. He walked down the steps and climbed into his Roadster and drove up river to check on the other citizens who lived on the river bank.

Chapter 2

Doug turned into the pull-over bright and early the next morning at 7:00am. Georgie stormed out onto the side deck, putting on his jacket and biting into a sausage biscuit. "Walk Georgie! The steps may be icy!" his mother yelled out the door to him. Doug's roadster was nice and warm when Georgie climb inside. "It's cold out there" he remarked, shivering as he spoke. Doug pulled out of the pull-over and drove down river toward Madison.

Georgie was amazed at the damage that was done by the flood. All sorts of trash and debris were left along the river bank. Doug slowed down so Georgie could have a good look at the house that was washed up and resting on its side. "Isn't that unbelievable?" Doug said as they drove past. Georgie had nothing to say but he kept his eyes glued to it at they travel on.

When Doug drove past the courthouse, men had already formed a line starting at it front doors, leading down the steps and on to the sidewalk, across the lawn and 200 feet on the sidewalk that circled the courthouse lawn perimeter. Doug found a parking space two blocks down Main Street. Georgie and he had to walk a good distance to get to work.

Doug introduced Georgie to the Jefferson County Treasure and he was surprised at how young he was. "Do you really believe he's able to do all of these calculations?" he asked Doug. "I only know what his parents told me" Doug answered. "But I know he's a senior at Madison high school" he explained. "I called the school yesterday afternoon and they told me he is making straight 'A's' in trigonometry." he continued. "I'll give him a trial, I'll check on the work this morning and if everything is correct….he'll be working for us" the Treasure said.

The Treasure lead Georgie to the desk he was to work at. It had two stacks of papers on it stacked at least two feet tall. "Does that much work brother you?" he asked the young man. Georgie looked up at the Treasure and calmly answered "No, not at all." He left Georgie alone at the desk and walked away but he was in much doubt that he could do the job.

Georgie did his job making notes on his pad. Two hours later, he got up from his desk and walked into the Treasure's office. "I need a new pad" he said. The Treasure looked at him in unbelief. "What?" he asked the young man, who was looking at him very seriously. "I need another pad to work on" he said again, showing him the one he filled up with figures, lines and arrows. "Eh, sure you do… Miss Cameron can get you one. Just ask her" he said and Georgie did an about face and found the secretary.

At noon the Treasure had Georgie take the rest of the day off. He asked Doug to pick him up at the library when his shift was over. After Georgie left, the Treasure had some one check the quality of his work. The young man's work turned out to be exquisite. The lady who checked his work was amazed at the job he did.

Doug found Georgie seated at a table in the library with at least a dozen books scattered around. "I've got good news" Doug said as he approached him. Georgie looked up from his book with a face that asked a question. "You have a job. They really like your work, down at the court house" Doug told him with a big smile. It was such a great thing to hear because jobs were so hard to get in the middle of the Great Depression. John Matthews hasn't worked in years. Georgie's family has survived so long on hunting game, gardening and gathering in the woods.

"Do you have a Library card?" Georgie asked Doug. "Yes I do" he answered. "Could you check out these books for me?" he asked. Doug didn't answer right away but looked at the books he wanted. They were all text books. "Don't you want to read a novel?" Doug asked him. "I need to study these for my job" he said. Doug helped Georgie carry the books to check-out. Then drove him home.

Chapter 3

On the way home Doug noticed how Georgie was absorbed in one of the books he borrowed from the library. "What'cha reading Pal?"

Doug asked his young rider. "It's a book about the bible" he answered. "Well, that's a good subject to be learning" Doug said. "Yup" Georgie said not looking up from the book. "What the book about?" Doug asked. "It's titled "Number in Scripture" by E. W. Bullinger" Georgie answered him.

The conversation went silent. Doug was amazed how a child, not even 13 years old was studying the deep matters written in the Bible. Doug slowed down when he saw what happen to a barn that was between the road and river. "That barn was standing this morning and now it's collapsed" he told Georgie. "My Daddy says the river can be a monster. He's right about that" Georgie said. Doug pressed down on the accelerator until he got back up to the speed limit.

"Do you believe in God?" Doug asked his rider. "Yes I do. How about you?" he asked. Doug hesitated but gave him an answer. "I do believe in God….But I don't do much with my faith." Georgie closed the book he was reading "Why not?" he asked. "Oh I don't know. I mean, I believe in God but I'm not that interested in all that church stuff. Ya know what I mean?" Georgie shook his head "No" and opened the book once again. "I know I should be more involved with the things of God but I don't. But I do help people" He said defending himself

****

After two weeks of working for Jefferson county, Georgie earned enough money to buy the parts for the family Ford. John rebuilt the old carburetor and it only took him an hour to do it and put it back on the engine. Doug gave the old Ford a jump from the battery in his roadster. John sat behind the steering wheel and after a minute he pushed the starter button. A puff of white smoke came from the back and the old family car came to life.

John took Georgie to work and back for two months but it came to an end when John got a construction job. Ground-breaking started on the new Indiana Army Ammunition plant in Georgetown Indiana. WWI Veterans were the first to be called to work. John served in the Navy so he was one of the first to be hired. It was so good for him to be working again with the Depression effecting the whole country. He hated the fact that his 13 year old son was the bread winner for the family.

The greatest problem was John had to drive 60 mile down river and be there at 7:00am. He hardly saw his family during the week because of his work. But he did have the weekend to spend time with them. He still considered himself blessed by God because some of his friends had left home and traveled to other states to find work leaving their families at home. So, once again, Doug had to take Georgie back and forth to work.

Georgie's skills grew beyond the Jefferson county boundaries. The Indiana sixty ninth district was now employing him. His reputation was saturating all of southeast Indiana. The Governor heard of Georgie's work and how smooth the flood recovery effort was going because of his competence. He sent Georgie a letter personally thanking him for his contribution.

Chapter 4

Doug and his wife Rita showed up at the Matthews church the following Sunday morning. It was an entirely different kind of service than what they were use to. The singing was more spirited, The message was more convictive and the people were very friendly. "Rita said she wanted to make the church her home church but Doug wasn't to fast to make up his mind. "We should try other churches first" he said.

Doug talked about Georgie to his wife about Georgie every day after work. It was the most talked about thing between Doug and his wife. Rita really want to meet Georgie so she invited him home for Sunday fried chicken after the service was finished. John allowed his son to go home with the Eaton's.

As soon as the Eaton's were home Rita went to the kitchen to heat her prepared meal and Doug went to his Garage to quickly finish a project. Georgie was left alone in the Living room, the walls were lined with bookshelves filled with books. Georgie felt like he was in Heaven with all the books. He walked along the perimeter reading the titles on the bindings of the books.

After he walked around the Living room once he noticed magazine on the coffee table. The title of one of the magazines seemed to leap off it's cover and strike Georgie in the eyes. "UC Berkeley" magazine. Georgie often read Berkeley was one of the best schools for Mathematics.

Georgie pick up the magazine and took a seat on the sofa. The photos of the university fascinated him as he turned the pages. Then he came upon a display page. UC Berkeley was offering a $500 reward to anyone who could figure out a problem the Math Department has been working on for 70 years.

When Rita entered the Living room, she saw Georgie with the magazine. "That's my old 'Alma Mater'" she told Georgie. "What is your degree?" he asked her. "I didn't graduate. I have one more year to finish my Bachelors' of Science" she sadly said. She quickly lifted her eyes and said that she plans on going back. "Georgie don't get me wrong, I really love Indiana. The schools here are great...but I went to Berkeley! The Cum Laude of all schools" she said and broke out with a giggle. Georgie had a little laugh with her.

Georgie asked Rita if she saw the ad in the magazine about the math challenge? She said she saw the ad but math was her hardest subject to learn. Georgie told her he wanted to enter the contest. He asked Rita if he could remove the page in the magazine and send in the entry form.

Georgie sent in the form along with a 50 cents entry fee. He received the question and the return form five days later. Georgie took his time figuring out the answer to the problem. He read a book about the subject matter the question was dealing in and he slowly dug in looking at the problem in many different angles. Two weeks later he sent the return form in with his answer.

An entire month went by without an answer from the University. Georgie figured that he didn't answer the problem correctly and Berkeley didn't have time to tell him that. He figured he would never hear from them. Then all of a sudden Georgie did get a huge letter from the University. Georgie removed the pages from the envelope and on top was a certificate that told him that he correctly solved the 70 years old problem. Georgie ran through the Ohio river valley jumping for joy.

The second item Georgie noticed from the envelope was the $500 check. Georgie quickly gave it to his Mom. The last thing, Georgie noticed from the envelope, was the greatest of all his rewards. Berkeley sent Georgie a free scholarship to attend their university. Georgie was elated

Chapter 5

John Matthews was dead set against his 13 year old son leaving home for California. "I spent some time in California when I was in the Navy" he said. "The West Coast is the craziest place in the world. Georgie will return home as a raving maniac" he told his wife. Georgie mother for once in her life said "no" to her husband's decision.

"Our son is going to college!" she said standing her ground. "John, Berkeley is the best school in the country for someone gifted like our son…. It's a scholarship! We don't have to pay it!" she pleaded. "Ruth!

he's only 13 years old….he can't live on his own….he needs to have parents to take care of him" John returned.

Ruth took time to cool off before she spoke again. When she gathered her thoughts she told her husband the latest news. "I was talking to Doug's wife Rita and she once attended Berkeley….she wants to finish getting her Masters degree there" she said. "If she is accepted is Doug going with her?" John asked. "Of coarse he's going with her!" Ruth laughed. John's gave her an angry look so she lost her smile. "Ruth, we can't pay them to watch our child" John objected.

Ruth looked at her husband, then looked at the ground, then looked back up at her husband. "She said she would let Georgie live with them and they would take care of him as if he was their own. We wouldn't have to send them a dime" Ruth said. "What does Doug say about all of this?" John asked her. "She says, he's fine with it." she told her husband. "What if he start to miss you and wants to come home?" John asked. Ruth looked directly into John's eyes "I know he will miss me, just as I will miss him but he's a lot more grown up than what you think" she answered her husband with conviction.

John paced back and forth across the room a couple of time, then he made his decision, "If Berkeley accepts her. Georgie can go" he said. Ruth put in hands in the air and ran and gave her husband a hug. "Thank you so much" she cried. "You are an understanding husband"

*****

That following Autumn, Rita and Georgie started their classes at Berkeley. The three of them arrived in California two weeks before classes began and Georgie was getting adjusted to his new home remarkably well. Everything about California was different from Indiana. The whether, the Floral and Fauna and especially the people. Georgie's father was correct in saying the people on the west coast were crazy.

One thing did rise up during the move, Georgie no longer wanted to go by the name "Georgie". From now on, he wanted to be called "George." He said "It's going to be hard enough at my age to fit into the college life. I don't want to be called a baby's name." George walked the Berkeley campass twice looking at the clothes the students were wearing. He was surprised to see the men not wearing ties and they were wearing their shirts opened at the neck. Georgie saw lots of "Boater" hats which at first he thought was comical but it was the style. He made a list of some of the clothes he thought would look best on him. The night before college started, Rita took George shopping to buy him new clothes. He paid for them with the money he earned working for the state of Indiana.

Doug got a job at the US Navy Operation Center in Alameda. He went to work the day after they arrived in California. The Navy also made military housing available for him til he found different housing. Rita and George were eight miles from the Berkeley but it wasn't a bad drive. Doug was so close to his work he could ride a bicycle. The exercise did him good.

Chapter 6

It wasn't long until the American Mathematical Society urged George to travel to Kansas City Mo. To be in a national math contest. Doug and Rita couldn't get a week off from their jobs to go along with him. But George was determined to go and the Eaton's wouldn't budge. So George went over their heads. He sent a wire back home to his mother in Jefferson County Indiana and she sent a wire back saying George was intelligent enough to do the trip all alone. The Eaton's took George to the airport reluctantly and he got on board a Ford Tri-motor "Tin Goose" and flew for the first time in his life. He closed his eyes and prayed during his entire trip to Kansas City. George had no problems finding his luggage and hoping into a cab to take him to the 21c Museum hotel where the contestants in the math competition was staying. The hotel was a very busy place that afternoon. There was three lines checking everyone in through registration. As soon as George was checked in, a Porter took up his large suite case and escorted Georgie to his room.

When he entered the room he noticed, he was sharing the room with another contestant, who was already checked in. The young man was sitting behind a desk practicing for the competition and when he saw George he rose to his feet and introduced himself. "Hello, my name is Ernst Orsic. I'm from Milwaukee Wisconsin....where are you from?" he asked. Ernst looked to be around sixteen years old. He was a very tall and blonde. A perfect example of a handsome Aryan type.

"My name is George Matthews" he told his new room mate. It was the first time he introduced himself as George, it made him feel like an adult "And I'm originally from a small town on the Ohio River in Indiana named Madison. The town hasn't changed in a hundred years.

The only thing different is people drive cars in town instead of riding horses." George said and it made Ernst laugh. They continued to talk about their home towns and schools. Ernst was very impressed at George attending U.C. Berkeley. "That's the school I want to go to" he told George.

The conversation went on and George continued to unpack, then Ernst mentioned he had a twin sister. "Emma is rooming next door, I'll introduce you to her later" Ernst said. "Is Emma competing in the competition?" George asked. "She's going to be my greatest competition" Ernst said. "She says sometimes the answers to problems just pop into her head….She's such a smart girl but she says silly things" he continued. George was taken back by what Ernst said about his sister. "Answers just pop into her head" George thought. "That just doesn't sound right" he kept thinking. He put the last things in the closet and the drawers. He tried to ignore what Ernst said about his sister but the thought just wouldn't go away.

Just as George put away his last pair of socks into the drawer, a big commotion erupted in the hallway. Ernst opened the door to see a young girl with a troop of hotel porters bringing her luggage to the room next door. The girl was Ernst's sister's room-mate for the competition. It was obvious the girl's parents were rich but she wasn't bossy or arrogant to the men helping her. She was tall and firm and she carried herself well. She wore fashionable clothes but they weren't high fashion and over priced.

Emma opened the door for her new room-mate and they introduced themselves. Instantly they began talking as if they were life-long friends. They spoke to one another a week ago earlier over the telephone and that was enough to bond them as friends. The porters were too busy to go inside the girls room. They left the luggage in the hallway by the door. Ernst told the girls that George and him could finish caring in the luggage.

"Susan, this is my twin brother 'Ernst' and this other gentleman I haven't met…." Ernst got the hint. "Oh! This is my room mate for the competition George. He goes to U.C. Berkeley. George turned around while lifting up the heavy suit case He saw Emma and thought he was looking at an angel. Unlike the dictates of fashion, Emma's golden blonde hair flowed down to her waist. Her olive complexion stood as back drop for her stunningly beautiful blue eyes. George felt romantic attraction for the first time in his life.

Susan Baxter was from Kingsport Tennessee. Her parents were on the board of directors of a world renown chemical corporation. Even though Susan was born and bred in the heart of Dixie, booth of her parents were from Great Britain so Susan only had a slight southern accent in her speech. Like his new room-mate, Ernst was attracted to Susan and the attraction was mutual between the two of them. "Let's all eat supper together" Ernst suggested, wanting a chance to know more about Susan. The girls looked at one another and laughed and shook their heads "Yes." George nodded "Yes" also.

The four of them ate supper at the hotel restaurant. They all sat at one table that was as far away from the rest of the tables. George felt very out of place being with them. Not only was he three years their junior, he was over weight. They tried to incorporate George in their conversation but he was unable to say much.

After supper was finished, the girls invited the guys in their room. Susan said she had a surprise for everyone. She took a pen knife and cut the strings on a box she brought from home. She searched through some books and magazines till she found what she was looking for. Susan lifted a bottle of home made Tennessee corn liquor over her head. "Surprise!" she said loudly and Ernst and Emma laughed. It was such a shock to them but it made George fearful and nervous. "Dad's secretary gave me this bottle" she said "She said it would be good to calm my nerves."

"George, go next door and get our two glasses from the bathroom" Ernst asked. And he responded without saying a word. Once he got to the bathroom next door, he looked at his image in the mirror. "That is the face of a Sinner" he thought to himself. The thought of staying in his room and not returning next door entered his mind but he paid no attention to it. He wanted to fit in.

The two boys sat on the beds as the girls came near to them with the two chairs in the room. Susan filled each glass half fill as they held it close to her and lastly she half filled hers Then the four of them lifted their drinks shoulder high. "Here's to the contest" Susan toasted they clanged their glasses together and Susan put the glass to her lips and turned it upside down in her mouth. The other three copied her but it wasn't the same. The corn liquor was like fire. Ernst and Emma put their classes down and were gasping for air. George almost vomited.

The more they drank the quieter it got, the conversation between them slow down but not for George. The liquor made him throw caution in the wind. He opened up with talking about the big flood on the Ohio River. The three of them listened to the many stories he had about it. The more they drank the more he talked. Next he talked about how backward the people in his small town were. He told funny stories of people doing foolish things that they wouldn't have if they only know better.

It was one thing to have everyone's attention but another thing to have Emma's attention. "She's laughing at my stories" he thought to himself. It made him feel so good to have her listening. They kept drinking and he kept telling stories till Ernst and Susan finally passed out drunk. George and Emma were alone, in a sense. It felt so surreal to George

Emma asked George to help her walk Susan to the bed he was sitting on. Susan muttered and stumble but they got her fall down on her bed. Next he took a place where she was seated. It was silent for just a second, then Emma spoke "You want to polish this off" she asked showing him the last two swallows left in the bottle.

George shook his head "No" She give him a happy smile "Suit yourself" she said and poured the content in her glass. "I'm going to let you in on a secret" she told George. His heart started pounding like a rabbits. She stared coldly in his eyes. George felt like a snake being charmed. Then she broke into a child-like giggle and George joined her. They both were very drunk.

When they came back to their senses, Emma stared at him once more with that cold look. "I'm not smart at all" she told George. "Oh don't say that. You couldn't have came here if you wasn't smart" he commented. "I reach outside of myself and get the answers" she said. George couldn't respond. "I get my answers from voices I hear that aren't of this world" she told him. George froze, he could do anything but look at her beauty. "She talks to the devil" he thought. Help me drag your brother back to our room" he asked. She helped him and when they finished they looked at one another face to face. "Good night" he said. "Good night" she said. Then she kissed George on the forehead and left.

Chapter 7

Kansas city Municipal Auditorium was filled to overflowing the next day. A desk for every contestant was set up in the arena for them to work from. All the students were presented with the same questions and they all worked on the question individually. They were also timed on how long it took them to complete the equation. But were even more graded for their accuracy in completing it. Lots of pressure was placed on the kids it was part of the contest.

None of the four corn liquor drinkers were ready to face the competition that was set before them. Susan knew enough to make herself vomit before she left the hotel room. The other three walked into the competition with sick stomachs. When the clock counted down to zero, one of the judges fired a blank bullet in a pistol and the contestants removed the ribbon around the questionnaire and began solving the problem. The four judges walked between the rows of desks making sure there was no cheating taking place. When the contestant finished the problem they raised there hand and the judge gathered their answer and their work sheet and marked the time it took for it to be completed.

George was the third person to raise his hand and around a minute later Emma raised her hand. George looked at her and gave her a thumbs-up and she smiled. One of the judges saw them and gave them both a sour look. The students had the entire morning to figure out the test and even if the contestants finished the problem they couldn't leave. They had to stay at their desks and be absolutely quite or they would loose points. No two students were allowed to go to the restroom at the same time. They had to wait for one another.

Poor Ernst's stomach would not settle down. An hour into the test, he ran from his desk to a waste paper can with everything in his stomach coming out. He was very lucky he made it to the can in time. The sound of him walking away upset everyone in the auditorium. The judge told him to drink as much water as he could keep down. "Son I can smell that you were drinking alcohol. That was very very stupid thing to do the night before the contest" he told Ernst. "I won't say a word to anyone as long as you straighten up and fly right" he said.

None of the four ate a thing during the lunch break. Ernst shared with everyone that his stomach felt better by drinking water. The other three took his advice and drank as much as they could. Because Ernst got sick he couldn't finish the first test. He wanted to totally give up on the competition after that. But his sister and two new friends talked him into remaining. "You will have this competition for your resume if you finish it" Susan told him. And it sounded like good advice to him. So he joined in the next test.

That test went much better. Emma breezed right through the question and felt very confident that she did well. She was the first to raise their hand. George was finished with his test two minutes later. This time they were careful not to make the same mistake with the thumbs-up thing. They sat quietly with their hands down on their desks staring into space, for the rest of the afternoon. Susan and Ernst did much better on the second test. Ernst felt lucky his friends talked him into staying in the competition.

After supper, the four of them met once again in the girls room. "Do you have another bottle of that Tennessee sipping whiskey?" Ernst asked Susan, with a smile on his face. The three of them gave him a very dirty look. He kept smiling. "I'm only kidding" he laughed. There was silence for a moment and Emma broke the silence saying. "I want to show everyone something" she said going to her drawer. She searched through her belongings and came out with a can of "Prince Albert's" tobacco.

"Oh come on, Cigarettes!" Ernst scoffed. Emma tossed the can in his lapped. "Open it up and smell" she said. Ernst did what she said. "This isn't tobacco. What is it?" he asked his sister. "It's Reefer" she answered. "Marijuana?" Susan asked loudly. "One hundred per cent" Emma answered. "Where did you get it" Ernst asked. "From Aunt Maria" she answered. "She gave me it before she returned to Germany" she added. "That stuff will make you insane. Didn't you see the movie 'Reefer Madness" Susan scolded. "Ah fewy" Emma answered. "That's balderdash! They wanted to scare everyone from smoking it during prohibition" she continued.

"Does anyone know how to 'roll-your-own? I tried it and I just made a mess" Emma asked. There was silence until George spoke up. "I grew up in tobacco country. I can roll one up" he said. Emma got excited "roll us up one, George" she asked. They all watched as George took the paper and folded it in his fingers and carefully poured the marijuana into it. He rolled it up using both hands and licked the edge. Then he sealed it between his finger and stuck it in his mouth. He pulled the joint out of his mouth moistening the entire thing. "George knows what he's doing" Emma remarked.

George handed her the finished product and she looked at him like he was a knight in shining armor. "Whose going to smoke this with me?" she asked. There was no response. "Oh come on you guys!" she said in dismay. "I will" George said. Inside he was scared too death to smoke with her but he had such a crush on her. Emma placed the joint in her mouth and stuck a match and put it to the end. She took a big drag and gave it to George. He took it and sucked it in and blew it out. "You have to inhale it George" she said while exhaling the smoke out of her lungs. George inhaled again. This time he did it right. He held it in.. "That's it George, good going!" she said taking the joint from him and taking another hit.

They shared the thing between themselves and Ernst and Susan watched. "Roll us up another one, George" Emma asked and he obeyed. Half way through the second one George exhaled and said "I feel happy. This is so much better than drinking" Susan asked to join them and they didn't refuse her. Ernst joined them with the third joint. For hours they giggled and spoke very loud. Telling funny stories and doing funny things.

Chapter 8

The competition went on and on, two tests per day. Emma or George were always the first to finish. A young competitor named Tony Shrum from Indianapolis would always be the third contestant to raise his hand. Tony and his room mate were neighbors to the girls, opposite from the boys. He was so angry for not doing any better than third place in finishing the examination. He constantly gave George and Emma dirty looks. They tried to be friendly to Tony but he wouldn't except their kindness "We may have finished before you but we may not be correct" Emma and George said to him over and over. Their words only made him more angry.

On the last morning of the contest everyone met in the auditorium for the winners to be announced. The big room was changed from being a classroom with many desks into a presentation room with rows of fold-up chairs. The contestants' friends and families filled the auditorium and there was some who watched from the foyer. The MC made a speech on the American Mathematical Society and all of things organization was involved in. He went on talking about the importance of Math and how the future is going to need more Arithmeticians.

Then the moment came for the winners to be announced. Emma was sitting next to George, she reached over and took his hand for support. She wasn't conscious that she did it but George anticipation turned from the winner to the excitement of Emma was holding his hand. "Third runner-up goes to, with a 95% on time of completion and a 92% on accuracy. Third place goes to Mr. George Matthews of U.C. Berkeley" He announced. George stood up and waved his hand at the crowd who were cheering him. He was happy he made third place, he wanted first place but it belonged to someone else.

Down the row from Emma and George sat Tony Shrum. He looked at George and gave him a shrewd look. It was a look that he was sure he was going to make first place. Second place went to a girl from

Foley Alabama. She scored 100% on accuracy and 90% on time of completion. She edged George out third by 1%.

Then it was time to announce be big winner. Emma squeezed George's hand and they booth looked into each others eyes. "With a 98% on time of completion and a 97 on accuracy. First place goes to…. From Milwaukee Wisconsin, Miss Emma Orsic. The crowd erupted and she waved. Her parents were in the crowd and they were so happy. It was a fine time for everyone but not for Tony Shrum. He thought some how, some way, Emma cheated and he deserved the title. Everyone of the contestants received a certificate of participation with their percentages written on it. The document would be a great enhancement to their resumes.

Chapter 9

Rita Eaton wanted so badly to go to the award ceremony but it was just too expensive to make the trip. She sent George a wire and told him how proud she was of him for getting a second place in the contest. To George's surprise, a journalist from the Madison Courier newspaper (George's hometown) came to cover the story. And even more of a surprise, he took George into the business office of the Municipal auditorium. Waiting on the phone for him was his mother. It was the first time for either one of them to use the phone. The Matthews' cabin was so far away from Madison there was no electricity there. A phone at the cabin was beyond belief. They booth felt like they were speaking before an audience so it was hard to say what they really wanted to. But just the fact that the conversation took place was a bigger blessing for them to imagine.

Emma and Ernst's parents adopted George for the rest of the evening. They ate supper at an up scale restaurant in Kansas city. Mr. & Mrs. Orsic bought George a new suit to wear to the establishment. It was one surprise after another for George. When the evening came to an end, Emma and Ernst told their parents they wanted to spend the last night back at the 21c Museum hotel with their new friends. Their parents understood their request.

Just like every night during the contest, the boys ended up in the four room. "Let's make a vow between ourselves to be friends forever" Ernst said sitting in the floor with his sister and friends. The three of them all agreed that the week would be one of the highlights of their entire lives.

They all raised their right hands and joined hands with their left. They pledged an oath to be friends forever. After that Emma took out the tin of Prince Albert and George rolled up two joints with the last of the reefer left in the tin. When they finished smoking the four of them laid down on the floor next to one another, their heads were all spinning.

Suddenly there was a noise at the door. The hotel manager unlocked it and walked inside along two policemen along and Tony Shrum. "Don't Move!" one of the officers shouted. The four math geniuses rose to their feet expecting the very worst to happen to them. George began to pray for mercy to himself. "Keep the door open and see if you can get a window open. I don't want that crap to get me loony" the other officer said.

"I stayed next door and I could smell that stuff every night over here. Every morning I would wake up feeling funny and it lasted all during the day when I was doing the contest" Tony said. "I found some butts in the ash tray" the first policeman said. "Put them in an envelope, that's all we need" the other officer said. "I'm going to take your award" Tony said to Emma as the police handcuffed her and lead her away. She began to weep knowing his statement would more than likely come true.

The four of them were separated in Men's and Woman's lock-up, overnight. The next morning, the Orsics' had their twins released out of custody. The Baxter's flew into Kansas City from Tennessee and got Susan out of jail. No one was there for George. He made his one call to Rita but it would take days for her to be able to do anything for him. He had to do his time alone in a place far away from every one he knew. George felt very abandon inside himself.

Doug went to work to see if the US Navy could help his young friend. He stormed the Navy research department to hire George to do math for them. Right at that time they were researching the use of nuclear energy. The goal was to build a submarine that could go for days or months underwater without resurfacing. After two weeks of going to bat for George, the Navy said they would contact the authorities in Kansas City to see if they could work out a deal. Doug wrote his young Pal and told him the good news and George wrote his parents and told them what Doug was doing for him. Mrs. Matthews told her friends at church who were praying for George. It was good news for a lot of people.

When Emma and Ernst's Aunt Maria in Germany heard of their arrest she worked as fast as she could to get to the United States. Germany was in the middle of occupying France and security was very strict going from one country to the next. Aunt Maria worked very hard and was able to get to London. She got on board *the Queen Mary 2* and headed to New York City. There she boarded a Douglas DC5 at LaGuardia and flew to Milwaukee. Emma and Ernst were there at the airport to greet her when she flew in.

Maria admitted to her brother and sister-in-law that it was she who gave Emma the marijuana. She told the parents, she was a gifted child like herself and she could project herself into a world outside of the five senses. A world much more intelligent than our own. A world yearning to communicate with mankind and give him knowledge that would make the planet into a better place to live. The marijuana was only an enhancement to get Emma to a place where she could communicate with this higher power.

Hans Orsic thought his sister absolutely lost her mind. "If I knew it was you, who gave my daughter that reefer, you would not be under my roof at this moment" he yelled at her. "I'm sorry you feel that way, Hans" she answered trying to make him feel like he was unreasonable. "How did you come up with that insanity?" he yelled again. "I inherited it from Grandma Gretchen" she answered. "Are you serious, Maria, she had to enter an insane asylum" he said. "She wasn't insane, people didn't understand her" Maria said. Hans began to pace back and forth across the floor. "Maria, I can't tell you what to believe but I refuse for you to fill Emma's head with such foolishness" he told his sister. Maria looked at the floor and thought about what her brother just told her "Okay Hans, I will say nothing more to her about her gift as long as she lives under your roof but afterwards, she's mine" she punched back. "Maybe she'll be grown up by then" Hans counter punched.

Chapter 10

Maria loved horses and she loved to ride them. Her best friend back home in Germany lived on a huge estate. Every time Maria got a chance to brake away from her everyday routine, she visited her and they went galloping into the country side. Her friend told her about a place sh once visited in the states. It was a tiny island in Virginia named Assateague and the little town next door named Chincoteague. On the island were mysterious miniature horses and Maria longed to go there and see them.

Maria nagged her brother Hans until he let Emma to go to Virginia with her. Emma was scheduled to be in court in Kansas City, along with her brother, in two weeks. She feared so badly that she would have to do some jail time. Maria said the little vacation to Virginia would do her a world of good. The only requirement was no marijuana. Maria and Emma made the promise. "No dope smoking on this vacation."

Maria and Hans were very close to one another growing up in Germany. Maria talked her brother into letting her and his daughter drive his 1936 Stutz Bearcat to Virginia. The car was like a European sports car. Two seats only and a convertible top. Maria and Emma drove down the highways with the top down. Both women's long blonde hair blew in the wind like two flags. They were stunningly beautiful, they looked like two sisters more than an aunt and her niece. And every where they drove men would turn their heads to catch a glimpse of them.

The tiny ocean side town of Chincoteague was as quaint as could be. The ladies roomed on the top floor of a downtown hotel built in the 1880's. It was an old establishment according to Emma but Maria said "in Germany it would be considered fairly new." They rented two bicycles, the next morning and took a ferry over to the island. They rode their bikes along the dirt paths and now and then they would spot a small herd of tiny horses. They watched the tiny creatures graze beside one another. It was a refreshing to just look at them.

Next they rode past the lighthouse on their way to the beach. And when they got there it was deserted. Emma spread the blanket on the sand while Maria got their sandwiches and sodas from the small cooler fastened to her bike. They ate their meal watching the waves breaking on the beach. When lunch was over they stripped down to their swim suits, they were wearing under their clothes. They laid down on the blanket beside each other and soaked up the sun.

A few minutes later, Maria broke the silence. "How are you doing communicating with the outside voices" she asked her Niece. Emma made some grumbling sounds and said. "I haven't tried it since I was arrested." Maria was disappointed "You have a wonder gift and you shouldn't let it sleep inside of you" Maria told her. "I'm not like you, Aunt Maria. I can't do it unless I'm smoking reefer" Maria looked at her and smiled "And that's a bad thing?" she asked. Emma didn't answer. "You know smoking a little bit of reefer is not going to drive you insane. That was a silly movie they made here in the states about marijuana" she said. "I know, I know.." she answered. "But remember we made a promise to Dad" she added. "I know...but don't close the Door" maria told her

Maria gave it a rest for a minute or to. "Emma, I'd like for you to return to Germany with me" she said. "After I get out of jail, maybe?" Emma answered. "No Emma. I want you to go with me now" Maria said. "I can't go with you back to Germany. I have to be at court...I don't have a passport and I'm a minor. Mom and dad would never let me go with you" she returned with a thousand reasons. "You'll never live up to your full potential if in stay here in the US" Maria told her. "Aunt Maria, it's impossible for me to go with you" She said. "Would you go with me if it was possible?" Maria asked. "I don't know….Maybe" she answered. "You can go to Germany, if you wanted to" Maria said. "Aunt Maria, c'mon don't tease me like that" Emma responded.

They both sat up on the blanket and looked at each other. Maria gave Emma a very serious look "I work for the Nazis" she said. Emma was shocked "They're our potential enemies" she said. "That depends on your point of view" Maria said. "I don't know...I don't like Politics" Emma returned. "Smart Girl" Maria said. "How would I get there?" she asked her aunt. "Leave that to me" Maria said. "Do you want to go to Germany with me?" she added. "I'll go to jail if I stay here" she answered. "Yes That may be true" Maria said. "What about dad's car?" Emma asked. "I have someone to take care of it...Do you want to go with me?" Maria insisted. Emma shook her head "yes."

The next day, Maria showed Emma how to roll her clothes and things up real tight and she stuff them in a sea bag. It amazed her how much could be packed away in such a small space. "We are meeting a gentleman for lunch. He is our ticket to Germany" Maria told Emma. "I don't want you to talk to him. If he asks you anything. Answer his question as briefly as possible" she said to Emma.

Around noon they met the man at a small open air market. They all three walked among the seafood for sale in open creates till they came to a walk up restaurant. The three of them ordered steamed crabs along with corn on the cob, green beans and baked potatoes. They sat at a picnic table and ate their meal. Not much was said while they ate. Maria and the man conversed mostly in German. Emma only knew a few words of the language even though her parents were from there. After the meal, they separated from the man and walked back to the hotel. Maria explained to Emma, they were going to meet the man again, at the same picnic table. He was meeting them there at midnight.

Chapter 11

There was a small chill in the air that night. Maria and Emma flopped their sea bags on the picnic table and waited for their ride. It was a very dark night and it startled the ladies when the man spoke "Nobody is following you two. We are safe to go" he said. They descended down a gang plank to a floating tie off. They loaded their sea bags into a flat bottom row boat and climbed on board. The old man followed next. He pulled the rope on the outboard motor until it started and they headed out to sea.

The old man followed the shore line north against a rough chop. The rowboat ascended over a strong wave and came down hard. Emma got completely soaked in the slashed. They cruised the shore line for a mile or more till they came to a huge rock on the beach. The old man turned starboard and headed out to sea. The farther they went to sea the quieter the ocean was. Emma turned around and saw the lights of Chincoteague way in the distance. For all she knew, it might be her last view of the United States. The thought frighten her

The old man stopped the boat and cut the engine. He got out a walkie-talkie and said something in German. Obviously, he was hailing something or some body. He spoke to Maria, in German he told her to look in a 45% angle to the left and she did so. Maria spotted what they were looking for. It was one quick blink of a light in the distance. The old man started the outboard and they headed toward the light. Half way there the old man repeated the action. He got on his walkie-talkie and requested another signal. There was one more blink that was only around 100 yards away.

A minute later they came upon the Conning tower of a German U-boat. The old man killed the outboard and took two oars and rowed the flat bottom boat where it was in line with the length of the submarine. The U-boat pumped the water from the ballast tanks and it rose to the surface with the row boat resting on it's outside deck. Soon a hatch opened and an officer climbed out and greeted the women. He disappeared back into the submarine with the two women and the U-boat took on ballast and submerged freeing the rowboat from it's deck. The old took the row boat back to shore. The women were on their way to Germany.

*****

The sailors had been at sea for weeks and it was very hard for them to keep their eyes from staring at the two beautiful woman. Maria had no problem being on board the boat filled with men but not Emma. She felt very uncomfortable at the men's quick glances at her. As quickly as possible the officer escorted the two forward to officer country. Where they would remain for the entire voyage to Germany.

When they reached the ward room that they were to be staying in, the bow of the boat lowered to go deeper from the surface. "Are we under water?" asked Emma. "Yes we are" Maria answered. "Are we going deeper?" she asked. "Yes" Maria answered "How deep are we going?" Emma asked. She started to panic and it showed by her heavy breathing. "Calm down. We are safe" Maria said. "I got to get out of here! You have to let me out of here!" she panicked. She was suffering from Claustrophobia. She kept breathing rapidly and started crying. "I gotta get out of here!" she cried. Maria hugged her but she fought away from her and ran out the door and down the passageway screaming "I gotta get out of here!" Some of the sailors caught her and gently held her on the deck till the Doctor got there with a sedative. He injected it into arm and soon she fell asleep. An officer carried her back to her ward room.

Chapter 12

Albert Einstein was scheduled to come to Berkeley and give a speech. There was no main topic for his visit but most of the people who were to attend was concerned about Nazi Germany. Einstein was a hero to George and he wanted to go see him, badly. The problem was seating to the event was limited. All of the seating arrangements were taken by Facility, Politicians and Business Leaders. After all the seats were distributed, only four seats were still available.

The university decided to hold a lottery and sell the seats for ten dollars each. One ticket winner would get two seats. Rita brought the subject up a the supper table the evening she found out about it. "Any way to make a dime, the university will come up with it" she said. "I'd like to buy a ticket" George said. "It's a fool's game, George!" she said. "But it's a chance for me to see, Albert Einstein" he said. "Ten dollars is a lot of money to be taking a chance on. It's a weeks wages for most people" she said. "I'd still like to take that chance" George said. "Gambling is ethically, wrong. A person is gaining from another person's lose. That should never be. In any transaction both parties should gain" Rita taught him. "I really want to see him. I have the money for the ticket. Would you buy me one. Please. You could come with me if I win" George begged. Rita couldn't resist his begging. "Alright, let this be a lesson to you. A fool and his money are easily parted" she told George, as she agreed to buy him a lottery ticket.

The lottery ticket she purchased for George came up a winner. Instead of being happy Rita was angry at the result. She was afraid

George would become a Gambler because of his win. She even thought about secretly giving the tickets away but she didn't buy them and they were not hers to give away. Besides, George wanted to see Albert Einstein so much and a loosing ticket would brake his heart and a winning ticket would be so uplifting for him.

Einstein's speech was mostly about his life growing up in Germany and the evil motives of the Nazi party. At the end of his speech, he opened up the floor for questions. Ten or more people stood up to asked him questions that was mostly about his life and the Nazis. When the last question was answered, Einstein asked his audience "Does anyone else have a question?" George stood up. The usher came to George with a microphone. "What are the practical applications of the photoelectric effect?" he asked.

Einstein was surprised to see a young man, ask him such a question. "I'd be pleased to answer your question   after the meeting is completed. Please meet me here on the stage at that time" Einstein said. Rita and George   stayed put after the meeting. They had to go through a body search by the secret service before they could meet with Einstein. The officers escorted the two out of the auditorium to the residents of the dean of the university. They past through the double doors of his 1880's Victorian style home. They walked into the Foray and past the winding staircase. The home was elegant Einstein,   the   Dean   and   a scientist named J. Robert Oppenheimer met the two of them, in the back parlor.   They were seated comfortably in sofas and chairs waiting for them to arrive. The room was brightly lighted from an elegant crystal chandler that hang from the ceiling. The back wall was cover with rows and rows of books. It felt like they were in a library, instead of someone's home.

Rita and George took a seat across from the three gentleman on a sofa and the Dean introduced them as the youngest and *excuse me* the oldest students at the university. The Dean went on to tell the scientists that Rita was George's guardian and they won the lottery to attend the meeting.

Einstein was interested in George because of his question. He quickly sensed George was no ordinary student but a child progeny of math. The conversation with George lasted an hour. Einstein and Oppenheimer flooded George with questions that he was able to give intelligent answers to. The math side of physics George understood well but the science side of it he had a little trouble in understand it.

Oppenheimer was surprised to discover he had such a genius on the same campus he worked at. "I want you to come work with me at my lab" Oppenheimer told George. "Do you have any problem with that?" he continued. There was the matter of George being arrested for smoking Marijuana. He told the scientist about the incident, staring at the floor with shame. "I still want you to come work for me and I will appear with you at your trial" Oppenheimer told him.

Chapter 13

Emma felt like she was in prison. She and her aunt were not allowed to leave the tiny ward room they were housed in. All she could do was read the King James Bible. It was the only book in English that was on board the boat. Maria told her to read the Gospels and the book of Acts, then start on the Old Testament.

Worst of all, she was only allowed to take one shower on the entire voyage to Germany. And she had to take a navy shower. Which consists of wetting yourself off and quickly turning the water off. Then lathering yourself with the soap. Then rinsing yourself down. Fresh water was very limited on a submarine. She had to go without shampooing her hair because her hair was too long.

Every night, in the wee hours of the morning, Aunt Maria would get out of her rack. She got out her note pad and ball-point pen. She lite a candle and stripped down naked. She sat behind the little desk and closed her eyes. Now and then her hand would move her pen across the page, she was taking notes but the notes weren't coming from her. They were coming from a force outside of herself.

When Emma was awake, she would watch her. It was such an unnatural sight to see and it was scary, Finally Emma asked what she was doing. "I am yielding myself to a power outside of this world. They want to help us make this planet a better place to live" Maria told her. "Do you really think that will happen? You're only one person" Emma asked her. "I once told you that I work with the Nazis. But I'm not alone, I'm in a secret society called the Vril. Working together we can change the world.

The thought of a better world was integrating to young Emma. "How does it work?" Emma asked. Maria gave her a puzzled look. "How do you put yourself in a trance, like you do?" she asked. "Would you like to try it?" her aunt asked. "Will it drive me insane?" Emma asked. "No it's perfectly safe" Maria answered. "I'd like to try it" Emma said.

Maria took the candle from her little desk top and placed it on the deck. "Take off all of your clothes" she said. "Clothes only block the power of their communication" she continued. Emma removed her clothing and they both sat on the deck with the candle between them. Facing one another, Maria said "Give me your hands." Emma reached out, over the burning candle and Maria took her hands into hers. "Breathe in deep" Maria said.

A minute went by while Emma kept taking deep breaths. Then it happened, A power like that of a rushing wind swept from Maria's hands into Emma. It was very strong and frightening. Emma pulled her hands away and started crying. "It's okay, you're safe, they want to communicate with you very badly" Maria told her. "I can't do this" Emma said. "You're a special person, they could do so much with you helping them" Maria said. "I don't think I can" Emma said. "You'll be fine. let's turn in for the night" Maria said. And they both went to their racks and went to sleep.

Chapter 14

The U-boat tied up at a berth inside a submarine bunker in Hamburg Germany. It was after midnight when the sailors were allowed to disembark the boat Emma and Maria were the last to exit only followed by the boat's captain. There was a greeting party waiting for the women at the top of the gang-plank. Three government officials and a young Germany girl, Emma's age, was there to welcome them. The three men greeted Maria speaking German but the young woman spoke English.

"Hello, you must be Emma. My name is Genevieve" she greeted. Emma was sleepy and cranky. "I need a hot bath. I've been wearing these sailor dungarees for weeks it seems" she complained. Genevieve smiled and said "We'll get you to your hotel room quickly"

The ladies were rush into a limousine and driven to a posh hotel in the city. Genevieve escorted Emma to her very fancy hotel room but she didn't notice how nice it was. Emma instantly jogged to the bathroom and turned the hot water knob to the tub. With out closing the bathroom door, Emma stripped off the dungarees and put her toe into the water filling the tub. When the water level and the temperature was right she climbed into the tub and sank her head into the water. Then she applied the shampoo. Next she laid back in the round backing of the claw-foot tub and closed her eyes. She was in   ecstasy.

A half hour later, Genevieve woke her up and poured a vase of warm water over her head to rinse off the shampoo from her hair. Emma towel dried quickly and staggered to the bed and fell into it. She slept like a rock for the rest of the night.

The next morning Emma rose up in her bed and noticed Genevieve sleeping in the bed beside hers. She saw her suit case that she wasn't allowed to have while she was on board the submarine. She walked to it and got some clothes of hers and got dressed. "You look nice" Genevieve said peeking outside of her blankets. "Thanks, I'm hungry, how about you?" she asked, brushing through her hair. Genevieve got up and got dressed and they both went downstairs to the cafe.

German coffee doesn't taste the same as coffee in the states, Emma thought as she ask Genevieve to explain the menu to her. When they both made their orders, they began to talk with each other for the first time. They began by talking about small things, like clothes, movie stars and big band musicians. Then half way through breakfast, Genevieve asked Emma a meaningful question "How much do you know about the Vril?" she asked.

Emma didn't feel comfortable getting away from teenage girl talk. "Only what Aunt Maria told me about it and that's not much" she said. "She told the party that you are very gifted" Genevieve told her. "I tried to connect to the outside power and it about knocked me over" Emma said. "That means it wants to communicate with you" Genevieve said. "Well it scared the dickens out of me" Emma said.

They talked about the Vril and making contact with outside forces for the rest of breakfast. Genevieve convinced Emma to try to communicate with the powers again. Some ladies in the Vril were planning to have a meeting that tonight.

Chapter 15

George fit right into the research team of Oppenheimer's. Even though he was years younger than the other members on the team. He easily blended into their conversations and their ideas. Oppenheimer's goal was to discover another form of energy besides coal and petroleum to power the engines of our world. He believed it could be achieved by rearranging molecules of uranium.

One night Oppenheimer walked in on George at the lab. He was there alone at his desk reading a book. He thought it was strange for the young man to be there after hours. "What are you reading, George?" he asked. "Oh nothing" he answered not knowing what the scientist would think of him if he knew what he was reading. "Oh, it must be something. You look very involved in your reading of it" he said. George shrugged "I'm reading the Bible" he admitted.

Oppenheimer was surprised but it didn't show. "I was raised Jewish so I know some of the stories" he joked. George put on a little smile and started back reading. Oppenheimer really liked George and he wanted to take the time to get to know him. "May I interrupt you?" he asked. George looked up from his Bible, "Yes" he said. "I may be getting too personal. But do you believe in God?" he asked. George was Leary about answering him so he answered with a question. "Do you believe in God, Doctor"

Oppenheimer was surprised to get a question for an answer. "To answer your question, I do believe in God" he answered. He continued "I believe in a higher power, something has to be behind all of life and all of existence. To believe that it all sort of fell into place is beyond how real life really works" he said. That made George smile because that's how he looked at it all.

"Have you read any of the Bible?" George asked. "I had a class in High School on the Torah. It's part of the Bible" he answered. "That's nice" was George's quick response and he left it at that. "I been reading the Bhagavad Git, lately. It's the Hindu scriptures" he said. George respond with "That's interesting" then he went back to reading his Bible. Oppenheimer asked no more questions.

The next morning as the team was gathered for their morning meeting, Oppenheimer filled everyone in on the latest news. He received a letter from Albert Einstein telling how he was giving a letter to sign from a colleague of his named Leo Szilard. The letter was going to be sent to President Roosevelt. In the letter was information of how Nazi Germany was close to developing a nuclear bomb and the US needs to get busy and develop the bomb before they do. The news came as a surprise to most of the team but it was no surprise for Oppenheimer who had studied at the University of Gottingen in Germany.

A few nights later, Oppenheimer was in his lab alone. Out of the corner of his eye, he spotted a book that George left on his desk. His first thought was to ignore the book but he could not let go of the curiosity. It didn't take long for Oppenheimer to walk over and pick George's book up.

The witness of the stars was the name of the book, by E. W. Bullinger. He thumbed through the book stopping from time to time to see what the subject was about. Apparently, God wrote his word in the stars, where men of old could teach their children about Him as the man pointed his finger at the stars as his guide. The book was not a simple one. It was scholarly written and Oppenheimer was very impressed that the author used Psalms 9:1 *The heavens declare the glory of God; and the firmament shewed His handiwork*. It was a verse, he remembered from his youth in Jewish school.

Chapter 15

It was December 7 1941 and Oppenheimer invited George to his house for an afternoon dinner. George attended church that Sunday morning with Doug and Rita and they drove him over to the Doctor's place. George was greeted at door front door by by the Oppenheimer's. wife and their seven month old son. Kitty introduced herself as George approached. Then she uncovered the baby's face by lifting up part of his blanket. "And this is Peter, our son" she told George

After the they ate they retired to the den where they discussed the war in Europe. The conversation was mostly between Kitty and Oppenheimer but they took time to schooled George on what was happening. And how things go, the conversation turned into one about God and religion. This was a topic that George could participate in. "It all seems so mystical" Oppenheimer said. "There is no science behind the existent of god" he continued. "Do you think it's a little far fetched that all of existence just fell into place, without some sort of intelligence behind it?" George asked.

Oppenheimer sat silently, then he looked at his wife, then at George. "Even Darwin himself said that it was *absurd* to propose that the human eye evolved through spontaneous mutation and natural selection" George said. "Maybe he meant it was a remarkable thing. The way the eyeball works" Oppenheimer said "Just like if you say you're going to kill the next guy who cut in line in front of you" he explained.

They debated the issue for another for fifteen minutes, Then the neighbor from next door ran into the Oppenheimer home. "I don't believe it. Turn on your radio." he cried. "What's going on?" Oppenheimer asked. "Just turn on your radio" he said again. Then the neighbor left and went to the next house.

Kitty turned the knob on the radio and tuned to the place where they could easily listen. NBC was broadcasting from Honolulu. The Den became so quite you could hear a church mouse. The broadcaster's voice wasn't the same, he spoke in a very serious manner. Japanese aircraft was attacking the US Navy base at Pearl Harbor. From the words coming over the air waves, the situation didn't sound good. "What on earth are they doing!" shouted Oppenheimer. He rose from his chair and began pacing the floor, listening to the news as it came in. "They will pay for this!" he kept shouting

The longer he heard the news the angrier he became. He paced the floor back and forth and Kitty tried her best to calm him down but it was no use. George actually got a little frighten at his rage. He started praying to himself because of the attack but most of his prayer was for Doctor Oppenheimer.

Then the radio voice announced a Japanese Zero dropped a bomb on the USS Arizona, Oppenheimer stopped in his tracks and looked to the ceiling "If there's a God in heaven I'm going to build a bomb that will wipe those tiny little islands of Japan completely off of the globe!" he shouted and turned and walked into his office. He slammed the door behind him so hard it almost came off it's hinges. George and Kitty dared not to interrupt him as he cooled down from his animosity.

George silently left the den and walked out the back door of the house into Kitty's flower garden. He took a seat on a bench and buried his head in his hands and prayed. The aroma of the flowers was very strong and George imagined that birds were singing to him. He ignored it and kept praying but the melody of George's feathered friends would not stop. "Be quite birds!" he yelled. And there was silence for about ten seconds. All the birds joined together in a natural choir and sang George a psalm.

Seconds later Kitty came outside and joined George on the bench. "Am I interrupting you?" she asked. "No you're fine" George answered. "I didn't want to disturb you if you were praying" she said. "No it's okay" George said. "George, I don't know if there's a God but when I'm troubled I come and sit on this bench. And I reach out with every thing that I am. Hoping to get some sort of response from God, if he's out there" she told George. "So, what do you think? Has He ever answered you?" George asked. "You're going to think I'm off my rocker but I come out here and things are pretty quiet but when I reach out the birds start chirping and it gets louder and louder. And it's like...they are singing to me" she said. A warm feeling rushed over George when he heard what she said. "George, could this be the way God is answering my prayer?"

Chapter 16

The meeting that night was held at a small forester's lodge near Berchtesgaden. It took three hours to get there by train but it was a very enjoyable trip for Emma. The German landscape was so different than in the States. The mountains in the background as they traveled was breathe taking.

Emma was introduced her Aunt's four partners who made up the Vril, Traute Blohm, Sigrun Kuenheim, Gudrun Jentzsch, and Heike Erhartdt. All four of them were gorgeous and the length of their hair was to their waist or longer. Emma was grateful that Genevieve came along to fill her in on what the women talked about. A very elegant table was prepared for them but there was much more than seven chair set up for the meal.

Half way through the meal the double doors were opened and two uniformed SS agents stood at attention next to them. Walking into the dining room, to everyone's surprise was Führer, Adolf Hitler himself. Hitler took a seat at the opposite end of the table facing Maria who was seated on the other end The two of them seemed to share the authority of the meeting.

After the meal was finish and the tableware removed. The servants lite a few candles on the table, next they turned all the other lights off. There was only enough light to barely see the faces of those seated around the table. Suddenly a cold chill swept across Emma and she was very uncomfortable being in the presence of the man who was a huge enemy of the United States. Even more frightening was communicating with forces coming from out there... It all didn't seem to be right.

Everyone sitting at the table was absolutely silent. Then all of a sudden Aunt Marie froze stiff in her chair and she leaned her head back. Like always, she held her note pad down on the table with her left hand as her right hand began writing messages. The speed she was writing wasn't normal. The pen she was holding fluttered across the page like the wings of a Humming bird. The rest of her body was as stiff as a board and her eyes were closed.

Emma was terrified as she watched her Aunt in the trance. Then Sigrun fell into a trance and burst out with a haunting moan. Then she began to speak in a foreign tongue and one of the officers with Hitler quickly turned on a small tape recorder. Ten minutes pass and both of the women fell out of their trances and all was normal. The German officers looked through the pages of notes that Maria took and none of it was written in a language they could read.

Soon Hitler and the German officers left the meeting without much said to the woman. They took the notes and the tape recorder along with them. And for the rest of the night Aunt Maria and her four partners drank wine, told stories and giggled like they were all teenagers. Emma couldn't understand any of what they were saying but she did seeing how much fun they were having.

But Emma wasn't all alone, Genevieve was there with her and they talked and she was excited. "I can't believe we were visited by Führer" she said all starry eyed. Emma didn't tell her how it scared her to death to see him. "What do you think is in the messages?" Emma asked. "Oh I can tell you right now what it is. It's instructions to build a flying machine." Genevieve said. "Aunt Maria knows nothing about machines" Emma said. "She doesn't have to. You saw how the force moved her hand" Genevieve said.

Genevieve went on to tell her one night the force put Heike in a trance and she spent all night drawing a picture of the craft. It was disk shape and the engine is unlike anything thing that has ever been built. "Every week the women come together and get more instructions to build this *flying saucer*, Führer calls it." Emma looked stunned "So it's being built right now?"she asked. "Yes and we have no idea where it's being built. That's a Top Secret" said Genevieve. The conversation about the fly saucers end and the girls talked about simple things until they left for their hotel room in town.

Chapter 17

Doctor Oppenheimer and George traveled to the Bonneville Salt Flats in Utah to observer the testing of a new aircraft fuel UC Berkeley was developing for the military. The fuel was going to be tested in a 1938 Hudson racer, that was a top contender in the Indianapolis 500 that year.

The experiment was mixing nitro methane with another substance to get higher horse power from the engine. The university hired a professional driver to pilot the racer. The diver had ten miles of prepared surface to drive the car as fast as it could travel. Using the normal fuel the Hudson racer reached a speed of 153 mile per hour on the first day of the test.

It was a very impressive sight for Oppenheimer and George to see the racer streak across the horizon at such a great speed. "Who would have dreamed a hundred years ago that man could travel so fast across the surface of the earth" Oppenheimer remarked. George was astonished but also sad "It's too bad they had to close the Indy 500 this year. It may never open again and I always wanted to see a race there and I never did" he laminated.

The next morning the different crews set up for the test. On every mile of the coarse an area was set up with movie cameras and three time keepers with stop-watches. The entire ten mile coarse was captured on filmed and timed at every station. Oppenheimer and George were allowed to be at station seven. The car would be at it's greatest speed at that point of the coarse.

The two Observers set their fold-up chair under the awning at station seven and listened to the event being broadcast over the radio. George sat with his paper pad and pencil to write down the times as they came over the broadcast. Quickly he would calculate how fast the car was traveling. He challenged himself to figure out the speed before the car got to the next mile station.

At the first mile, George figured the car's average speed with 140 mph a far cry from it's high speed of 150mph that it reached the day before. Everyone knew the reason for the slower speed was the car was coming from a dead stop but all the next station he will be in motion. And his speed will be much greater.

At station number two, George heard the time come over the radio and quickly he made the calculation. 162 mph. Everyone at the station cheered when he announced his finding. The car's speed kept increasing at each of the stations. George heard the time at station six and like lighten did the math "197mph, he's going to go over 200mph before it's over!" George shouted. He jumped out of his seat and looked to the left and saw the car approaching.

Everyone could hear the roar of the engine as it shot closer to them. Two tongues of fire were spewing out of the exhaust pipes as it came near. The time keepers got their watches ready and the car crossed the seven mile mark and they clicked their watches off. All of a sudden, the most horrible thing accrued, the Hudson racer exploded into a giant ball of flames and debris flew all over the coarse.

The camera operators looked up from their eyepieces to see if what they were viewing was really happening. Everyone at station seven was stunned and silent. No one could move and even if they could, what could they do? The flames from the race car was burning at least ten feet high. The lead man of the timing crew got on his walkie talkie and told the officials at the starting line what had happened. The broadcaster announce to the other nine stations what had happened.

Oppenheimer looked at his young partner with a tear hiding in he corner of his eye. "We're going to have to do better than this" he told George. "This is our fault, we are the reason this happened" George answered with his eyes swelling up with tears. "We were as careful as anyone could be" Oppenheimer said to George. "We didn't do our math correctly, we're at fault" George said.

Oppenheimer went to George and gave him a one arm hug from the side. Then he stood in front of him and looked into his tear-filled eyes. "You did your job the best you could, you aren't to blame for what happened" He told George. "But a man is dead!" George yelled. "He knew the risk, George" Oppenheimer told him. "I don't think I can do this job anymore" He said.

Oppenheimer looked again into George's eyes. "Just a few days ago, we entered a war against Germany and Japan, your country needs you" he said. "The race car driver was killed doing his part for us to win this war. Maybe, George, with you doing your part, not as many lives will be lost" he spoke on. George's tears dried and he looked up from staring at his feet. "I guess you're right" he said. They folded up their chairs and drove home.

Chapter 18

It was a warm summer day when Emma and her aunt took the day off and drove into the mountains. They cruised with the top down on Maria's Porsche. The ride was a healing balm for the soul. The sun was in their faces and the wind blew through their golden Blonde hair. The air was so clean in the mountains, so different than in the city. Emma breathed in the good air as the bad air exhaled out.

Maria parked the little convertible at the roadside by an open meadow that looked down on the Neuchwanstein Castle. Her and her niece unloaded a blanket and basket from the trunk and walked to the center of the heath. Emma spread the blanket upon the ground and they took a seat in the center. Maria took out two glasses and filled them with white wine. They kicked off their shoes and sipped the fruit of the vine.

"We are special people, Emma" Maria said as she handed her a Bierock, she retrieved from the basket. Emma excepted the pastry without saying a word. "You are Aryan. You are part of a master race" she told her niece. Emma stayed silent. "The people of the world are a mess and it's always been that way" Maria explained. "They starve to death, they war against one another, they pray to foolish gods. The world is a wreck" she went on. Emma still stayed silent. "Us Aryans need to take the world over and cure this planet once and for all. That's the Nazi plan" Maria said.

"I don't believe that for one second!" Emma shouted at her aunt. Maria was taken back. "Living in he USA has ruined your thinking" she said. "I've grown up with people with different nationalities and cultures. I know what people can be when they are free to pursue their dreams!" Emma yelled. "When our people were writing symphonies, building Cathedrals and exploring the world. Others were running through the jungle, naked, throwing spears at monkeys" Maria shouted back. Emma turned her face and looked at the valley below. "Let's talk about something else" she said. Both Maria and Emma tried to forget their disagreement and continue the day without any hard feelings. It took an hour or two but things were a lot better between them before the day was over.

That following Monday Maria and Emma boarded a train for Paderborn. They were traveling there to visit Heinrich Himmler who was Adolph Hitler's number two man. When they arrived, they were greeted by a Gestapo officer driving a Daimler Benz staff car. He opened the rear door and escorted the women into the rear seat. Every eye in town was trained on them as they drove through town headed for the Wewelsburg castle.

The castle's staff was waiting in the foyer when the ladies arrived they were greeted with smiles and lead to a wing of the castle that was renovated for overnight guests. Emma and Maria got their own individual suites to spend the night.

Emma relaxed after a long days travel with a hot bath in the giant tub the room provided. She dressed in her best suit of clothes afterwards and joined Maria for supper in the huge banquet room downstairs. The two woman were seated at the head of the table at Himmler's right and left. Emma felt honored but also uneasy, it was a Nazi gathering.

After dinner everyone followed Himmler to the north tower. Himmler acted as a tour guide explaining all the renovation that had taken place since the Nazis rented the castle seven years ago. Maria translated to Emma the story of the castle as they followed Himmler. The castle was almost in total ruins before the Nazis restored it. Now the old structure was fit for royalty.

When Himmler finished his presentation, the lights were dimmed and he ordered every one to remove their clothes. Emma didn't understand his language but she saw what was happening and it made her very afraid. She watched Maria and her four Vril partners strip off all their clothing down to their underwear. Then she turned and noticed every one in the room had stripped down to their underwear. Maria noticed that Himmler was looking at Emma with an angry look. She went to Emma and told her to get undressed. Emma refused at first but Maria finally talked her into it. Like everyone in the room she stripped down to her underwear

Then Himmler lead his guests to what is known as *The Crypt* which was a sunken circular portion in the floor with a stone platform surrounding it for people to sit on. Maria walked to the center of the crypt and stood on a symbol of *The Black Sun* inlaid into the floor. She slowly turned as she spoke to the crowd that was sitting around. Making them feel like no one was more important than anyone else everyone was equally important. Then Maria started to chant some words in German and everyone joined her. Emma tried her best to chant the same words as everyone else but it was hard to distinguish the words with everyone speaking at the same time

A tingling presence came over Emma and all of a sudden she felt herself being lifted from the stone bench. She was being levitated by a force outside of this world. The people in the Crypt began chanting louder and faster as she floated around the room. Emma felt like she was drunk or on some kind of drugs. Her whole body was as limp as a noodle, she should have been screaming in fear. But she just floated along in thin air, numb to the world.

When she circled the room once, she began to rise higher and higher. And one of the woman stood and started to do a very loose and slow dance. She turned in circles and moved her arms like two snakes crawling on the ground. Then other woman joined her doing a serpentine dance. Some of them imitated her but others got even more exotic.

Emma floated high and higher in a seated position, then the force made her sit back like she was lying flat on her back. Next the force flipped her over where she could see the women dancing beneath her. They stopped dancing and formed a circle. They raised their hands into the air and looked up at her. Then they began to chant something different in German. Emma closed her eyes for a second and when she opened them, she was traveling in outer space at the speed of light.

She came to the constellation of *Alpha Tauri* and slowed down and the planet *Aldebaran* appeared. Then she landed into what seemed to be a town square where a crowd of beautiful humans cheered her arrival. It was like she did something great or heroic. As they applauded her, four young Aryan men gathered her up on their shoulders and began walking to what looked like a futuristic cathedral. The crowd followed them, still cheering as they went. It was all too much for Emma to imagine, she raised her head back and past out.

Emma woke up and was back at the c*rypt*. Maria was sitting next to her when to came to. "Did you see me leave?" she asked her aunt. "You had a vision" Maria told her. "So I never really left this place?" she asked. Maria shook her head *no* and smiled. "It seemed so real, it was like being in heaven" Emma said. "You are being called to do great things" Maria told her. Emma was stunned. "Let's get dressed and return to ours rooms" Maria said

Chapter 19

Oppenheimer heard a knock on his front door and when he answered it, an Army officer was standing before him. "Doctor Oppenheimer?" the Officer asked. "Yes" he answered. "The President of the United States needs to see you as soon as possible" he said. "My goodness, what's this all about?" the doctor asked. "It's Top Secret. You need to come with us as soon as possible" the Officer said again. "I need to pack some clothing and tell my wife" he told the Officer. "Tell your wife and everything else you need will be provided" the Officer told him.

Oppenheimer found Kitty in the back yard taking care of her flowers when he and the officer told her, he was needed by the President. They both did an about face and left Kitty dumbfounded. George was coming to visit the Oppenheimers for a second time. As he approached the Oppenheimer's home, he saw the Professor and the Officer drive away in an Army staff car. George saw Kitty standing at her front door watching the two of them leave. He approached her and asked "What's going on?" Kitty shook her head "President Roosevelt wants to meet with Rob" she answered. George shrugged and asked no more questions.

The Officer drove Oppenheimer to Travis Army Air Base and they board a B24 for Sheppard AAB near Dallas Texas. There they boarded a B17 and flew to Arnold AAB near Nashville Tennessee. They then boarded another B24 and flew to Andrews Army Air Base near Washington DC. The entire trip took 20 hours and Oppenheimer was exhausted when it was finished.

Oppenheimer met with President Roosevelt the following the following afternoon. The President told him about the secret operation the Government was planning to establish named the *Manhattan Project*. "We need to develop an atomic bomb before the Nazis" Roosevelt told him. The Doctor was surprised when Roosevelt asked him the be a leader of the project. The President said it would to be a joint effort between military and civilian personal. He went on to say "it would be best if a civilian was in charge of the civilian side of the operation

Roosevelt also asked Oppenheimer to find a location for the complex to be built. The site had to be isolated but have acceptable transportation both to and from the site. It should be far enough inland not to be bombarded from a naval attack. And as much as possible it should have a natural surrounding where it would be hard to attack on land. Both Oppenheimer and the President said between themselves that such a place may not exist.

When Oppenheimer returned back home, he was totally drained of everything inside of himself. Being in charge of such a project was entirely beyond anything he had every done. He never lead more than four or five members in a lab. How could he be a leader of hundreds? There was also making the bomb itself. Should mankind have such a bomb? Could the bomb be so powerful that it destroys the entire earth? And where should this site be built? These questions tormented him on his flight back home from Washington.

"It's time for me to get away from all of this" he told Kitty as soon as he got home. "Where do you want to go?" she asked. "As far away from people as I can get" he told his wife. "And where might that be?" she asked. "New Mexico" he said. "I've never been there" she answered. "For four summers I went to a school for boys called the Los Alamos ranch school. I'd like to go near there." he said. "Tell me more" Kitty said. "It's a beautiful place with mountains and deserts. There's a stream that runs through there and an accent Cliff-dweller Indian site. You can go horse back riding for hours and see different things around every bend of the trail" he said. "Sounds great to me. When can we leave?" she asked.

George had a way of getting what he wanted. It had been over a year since he had seen his parents and they were planning to come out to California to visit him. But at the same time The Oppenheimers were going to New Mexico. George wanted so much to see his Parents but he also wanted to go with the Oppenheimers.

John Matthews, George's Dad, was stationed in San Diego in WW1 and he hated California. When George told him he would rather meet them in New Mexico, he was all for it. John And Ruth were country people, who didn't feel comfortable in the city. Camping out in the mountains would be a much better get-away than staying in a motel or lodge.

The Matthews along with the Oppenheimers camped on White Rock at overlooking the Rio Grande River Valley. It was the perfect spot to pitch a tent and go horse-back riding. Oppenheimer rented the five horses from his old school master at the Los Alamos Ranch School. Oppenheimer and John Matthews had the best time together. They both had a love of nature and living like pioneers.

John told Oppenheimer about his cabin home in Indiana, set high above the Ohio River. He told him about the riches of the wooded hill side. Hunting rabbits and squirrels to kill and eat. Gathering nuts and berries, mushrooms and Polk salad. He told him about fishing in Eagle Hollow creek, of catching Bass and Bluegill. Catfish and Crappies. John explained how he put a garden out down by the river after the rainy season was over. How he planted rows of corn and tomatoes. Beans and cucumbers, squash and peppers, watermelons and turnips. The land was rich for growing a corp and John took advantage of it. Oppenheimer decided that he must visit the Matthews someday to see how all of this was done.

At the camp fire that night, Oppenheimer told some of the stories he heard when he attended the Los Alamos Ranch school. Most of the stories were about Indians and Indian legend. Some of were heroic, some were scary, some were funny but all of them were told with all the color and imagination Oppenheimer could muster up.

The Matthews turned in early, George crawled into his little pup tent and Mom and Dad in Theirs. The Oppenheimers stayed by the fire and drank hot cocoa. After the Matthews had fallen asleep they both started a conversation. "I think John and Ruth are a remarkable couple, don't you?" Kitty asked. "I can see, they miss being with their son" Oppenheimer said. "I saw tears in Ruth's eyes when she first saw George" Kitty said. "Don't let me forget to tell them, how much George is needed by his country" Oppenheimer said. "I need to thank them" he continued.

They both kept staring into the flames of the fire, drinking their cocoa when Oppenheimer interrupted the silence. "John is a praying man, he prays all the time" he said. "I saw him this afternoon, when we all finished the ride. He climbed a tall rock and prayed there" he added. "Some people need to believe in God and it does them good" Kitty remarked. "You're going to think I'm silly but I wanted to join him, up on that rock" Oppenheimer admitted. "Oh C'mon!" she expressed.

Oppenheimer smiled "I'm not saying that I believe in prayer, it just looked so peaceful" he explained. "I am so bewildered where to locate a site for the *Manhattan Project*" he went on. "Try not to think about it, you're on vacation" Kitty told him. Oppenheimer agreed and took another sip of cocoa.

Then a thought come to Oppenheimer's mind, it was like he was struck by lightening. "It's right here, Kitty!' he said loudly. "What are you saying?" she responded. "The *Manhattan Project*! We could locate it right here! It's a perfect place! It's isolated, It's far from the coast! There's already a road to drive up here! And a railway down town! And it's so beautiful here!" Oppenheimer kept rumbling. "And we might be able to purchase the ranch school" He said. Then Oppenheimer got a strange feeling, like an inclination, *God spoke to me*, he thought. It was so overwhelming and he believe it. He remembered in college reading the Bhagavad Gita. The idea came to him to read it again.

Chapter 20

Maria got word the Nazi command wanted her and Emma to go on a secret mission. They were not told where they were going, only they would be absolutely safe and well taken care of. They had no problem taking the Nazis up on their offer. Three days later they boarded a train and traveled to *Bremerhaven* Germany in a first class luxury car. They stayed in the finest hotel in the sea port city. Maria and Emma both enjoyed their own opulent suite that overlooked the bay. The next morning they ate a fine breakfast. They both ordered an open faced Laks og eggerore with ansjos, the two of them love the dish

The staff loaded the ladies luggage in a military staff car while they ate. After breakfast they were driven to the piers and the staff car parked beside a huge ship named the *MS Schwabenland*. Two Gestapo officers escorted the women onboard the ship after they exited the car. The officer escorting Emma was a very attractive, an Aryan blonde. He was tall and built like a Greek God. But he had a boyish smile that made Emma heart rate go up.

Traveling on a ship was so different than from being on a submarine. Emma was able to wander on the upper decks and get plenty of sunshine and fresh air. Her and her aunt ate their meals with the officers. The meals were simple but they tasted good. Once she had the opportunity to sit across the table from her handsome escort. It was a good time for her to practice speaking in *German*. She talked with him and his friends, she only mispronounced a few words.

Best of all Emma could take a daily shower. Knowing, all the fresh water had to be made from sea water. She showered quickly but it was so much better than the weekly *Navy* shower she took on the U-boat. Her Aunt didn't care about the amount of water she used she took as much time as she wanted to in the shower. Emma said sometime to her but she ignored her.

Days turned into weeks and there was nothing to see from the ship but water. The captain would turn the ship to avoid getting close to another ship. They never told the women where they were going, all they knew was they were going south in a zig-zag pattern. Emma and her Aunt spent the majority of their days sitting in deck chairs, reading novels and practice speaking German. The only other thing for them to do was jog around the forecastle and do calisthenics. As long as they stayed out of sight, all went well.

Then one afternoon, Maria rose from her novel "I can't stand this any longer, day after day I sit in the sun but I can't let it touch my skin, I can't get a tan!" she said, rising from her chair and throwing the book on it. "Come with me, Emma" she said to her niece. Emma followed her below deck to her state room. She opened her suitcase and took out her swim-suit. "Go next door and get yours" she commanded. Emma didn't question her, she did what she was told. When she returned, her aunt was in her swim-suit. "You look like the Betty Grable pinup" Emma said. "I'm better looking" Maria answered laughing.

They both put their sailor dungarees on over their swim suits and headed back up to the Forecastle. Once they were up there. They kicked off their dungarees, laid back and soaked up the sun. It felt so good to them to be taken in the sun. They applied sunscreen to one another, if they got a bad sunburn and the Doctor would have to see them and the Captain would restrict them in their quarters.

All of a sudden something fell on the deck and made a noise. It was only a tool that fell and the noise wasn't loud. But the women jumped up like a bomb stuck the ship. They hid themselves the best they could with their towels but it covered little. Then they saw high upon the mast, a sailor working on something, his head was turned. He spoke in something in German and Maria began to laugh. "What did he say?" Emma asked. "He wants permission to come and get his wrench" Maria answered while she walked over and picked up the tool. "Come down and get it" she said in German.

The poor sailor's eyes were glued to the women as he climbed down from the lofty mast. "Pay attention to what you are doing. I don't want you to fall" Maria said giggling. "Come and get it" she said to him when he reached the deck. Before he got close enough to get the wrench, Maria drop it on the deck inches from her feet. Then she flung off the towel she had tucked around her waist. The sailor picked up the wrench and panned his eyes up Maria's long legs, he was in shock. When he stood up straight, he did an about face and walked away. Maria giggled as he went. "You're terrible Aunt Maria!" Emma said. "It'll be a good story for the men down below" she answered.

After thirty days of being out to sea the air began getting much cooler and finally the women were told the ship's destination was Antarctic. They both were disappointed because they were expecting an exotic island in the Caribbean. The question now was "Why Antarctica, it's one great big ice cube?" They asked but never got an answer. As they got close to the destination, the temperature was as cold as the coldest days of winter in Germany. It was the middle of July.

At supper time in the Officers Mess the women were approached by two young officers. "We both are Pilots, would you two like to take an airplane ride tomorrow?" they asked. Before Emma could answer, her escort onto the ship said "You'll be flying with me" Emma was mesmerized "Ah...I'd love to go..." she stuttered. Aunt Maria smile at her because she saw how Emma was attracted to him.

After breakfast the next morning the woman put on lots of foul weather gear. All that was left exposed was their eyes but they had goggles to put on. The women climb on board the back seats of the two sea-planes on the MS Schwabenland. After they were buckle in and a short count down the planes were catapulted off the fantail.

Even tough it was a bright sunny day the temperature was only 10 0 F. The flight was fascinating, the ice formation were incredible. The plane swooped down and scared a raft of penguins on an iceberg. They dove into the water and jetted away. A minute later they saw two Poplar bears swimming in the drink. The two planes circled around them so the woman could watch.

Then they flew farther south, Emma's pilot began pointing at something for her to see. Seconds later she saw what he was pointing at.

It was a military camp with two U-boats berthed in the water. Emma figured it out, this was where she was going to be living. What a *desolate* place she thought. Then they flew back to the MS Schwabenland and landed in the water. The crane lifted both planes out of the water individually and set them back on deck.

Chapter 21

The government purchased the one hundred and thirty two acres and the building of the Los Alamos Ranch School. The project was a shared effort between military and civilian scientist and personal to build the atomic bomb before the Nazis. Oppenheimer's reason for the bomb was to prevent it from being used if the Nazis did develop one. "No weapon of this magnitude should ever be used" he told all the personal who were responsible for developing it.

Oppenheimer was the man in charge of the civilian side of the operation while Lieutenant General Leslie Groves was in charge of the military side of the project. The two of them did not see eye to eye on many things and plenty of time was wasted because of it. They were in constant battle over who should have the final authority. But surprisingly plenty of things got accomplished in record time. Laboratories, roads and home sprang up like mushrooms.

Doug and Rita Eaton were called by Oppenheimer to be a part of the Manhattan Project. Doug was an expert in Logistics and he already had a government clearance. Rita could be a school teacher for the children. And George could continued to be an assistance of Doctor Oppenheimer.

They were blessed to get a preexisting home there, these home had a bathroom with a tub. None of the new houses were built with tubs in them. The homes on the old street became known as *Bath Tub Row*. One week after George arrived at Los Alamos, he got a huge surprise. Ernst Orsic, his room mate during the math competition from Milwaukee, came to work at the Project. George was pleased to find out that Ernst didn't have to do any jail time because of his Marijuana charge but he had to do a ton of community work.

"What about Emma? Did she do any time?" George asked. "George...this is between you and me, only. Emma slipped out of the country with my Aunt Maria. They went to Germany" he told George. "But how....?" Ernst interrupted him saying "It was just before the war broke out" George looked more sad than he looked surprised. "Where is she at in Germany, what city is she living in? Is she safe?" George had a dozen questions. "We don't know. She has to keep it a secret" Ernst answered. "Why would she do such a thing?" George complained. "She thought, she was going to jail" Ernst answered. George became very depressed because of the news about Emma. He prayed a little prayer for her every time she entered his mind.

Other people came to Los Alamos the same day that Ernst arrived but George didn't get to meet any of them. He was really busy working in the lab with Doctor Oppenheimer. George went to the chapel on that following Sunday morning and half way through the service, he saw some one from the corner of his eye that looked familiar. George kept an eye on him and when the service was over he followed him outside. When he caught up to him, George looked over and saw it was Tony Shrum.

"Tony" George said and he looked over and a guilty look appeared on his face. "I'm so sorry for doing that to you guys at the competition, George!" he laminated. "Think nothing of it, we haven't smoked dope since then. It taught us a lesson" George said. "I'm a changed man....I've given my heart to the Lord" he said. "That's great, it's really getting hard for me to find college age people like us who believe in God" he said. "I have that problem too" he responded.

Oppenheimer had all three of the young men working in his lab one week later. Ernst, Tony and George all were working for him. He said he would rather have these young men working for him because they didn't argue with him. And they did what they were told. They asked him a ton of questions but he didn't mind. Being a teacher was his favorite job.

Chapter 22

The walk from the ship to the Main building of the secret military scientific base was treacherous. The cold wind was so strong it was hard for the women to stay on their feet. And the walk so far. Even though they were dress for the trip, there was still exposed parts of their skin that made the journey painful.

Nazi Base 211 was located in New Swabia territory, it was like a city under the ice. Hundreds of people lived and worked there comfortably. It was nice to see women working at the facility, There was even children there on the base. The journey on the ship made Emma feel like she was living in a goldfish bowl. She felt eyes on her even if she didn't see any one staring. That incident on the forecastle with the poor sailor dropping his wrench, didn't help either. It effected her so much that she stopped sunbathing with her aunt.

Thanks to Aunt Maria and Genevieve, Emma was able to speak enough German to get by. During the voyage to Antarctic she tried her best too only speak German. She made it her quest to continue to speak the language while she was at the secret base. *The more I learn the language the more I will know what they are saying to one another. And the more conversation I can have,* she thought to herself. It was lonely only having Maria to talk to.

When Emma found out the pilot who took her on the flight was going to transfer to the base, she about jumped out of her skin. A strong chemistry flowed between the two of them and everyone could see it. She tried her best to eat her meals at the same table with him but it happen that way. Otto Shoenheit, was always a Gentleman, his smile melted Emma. His eyes were adorable especially when he spoke to her. While on the cruise many of his friends grouped around him before she able to take a seat. She knew why, it was against regulation for an officer to fraternize with a civilian while the ship was under-way.

But this secret base was different because half of the population was civilian scientist and some of those regulations weren't enforced as much. She was able to sit directly across from him at supper time on that first night. She could not control her emotions "I am so happy you have transferred here" she told him smiling from ear to ear. All of Otto's finds looked at him and smiled.

After the meal, a group of officers and scientist escorted Maria and Emma to the main hunger, Otto went along also. When they entered through the door, they were able to see an incredible sight. Standing before them was a giant disk shape contraption. "This is our Haunebu flying war craft. The officer, tour guide, told the women. "It's absolutely magnificent!" Maria exclaimed. It was a spooky sight to Emma. The flying Saucer was a hundred thirty seven feet in diameter. It had a machine gun turret on top, in the center. It had Two machine gun turrets below and in the very center, of the bottom, was bomb bay doors

"Traveling in any direction and following the curvature of the planet, any target on the face of the earth could be bomb within two hours and what a hiding place we have here" the Guide said. Emma got sick to her stomach, the thought of the United States being so vulnerable was frightening.

After the tour, Otto approached Emma "I'd like to invite you for some coffee at the cafe" he asked Emma. Emma said sure but she was not as excited as she should have been. The capabilities of the Nazi flying saucer was still on her mind. They both ordered some decafe and sat in a booth opposite one an other. "Something is bothering you" he stated. She did not speak. "You can tell me" he said. Then she spoke. "I'm an American" she told him. "I'm aware of that" he said. "That flying machine could ruin my country" she said. "We wouldn't do that. The USA has so much going for it" he said. "We just need to change the minds of the America's people" Otto said.

"The Nazis want to take over the world" she said. "Well, yes, in a sense" he answered. "What makes Hitler any different than any other conquer in history?" Emma asked. "We have come so far since then" he said. "We want to end all wars and make the earth a better place to live on" he continued. "All conquers say that but look what really happened" she said. "But we have evolved" Otto said. "Balderdash! Evolution is balderdash!" she said loudly. "You saw our flying machine. Do you think mankind hasn't come a long way since antiquity" he stated.

"There's nothing new under the Sun, the Bible says" Emma responded. "Oh for crying out loud! Do you believe in a Christian God?" he asked with a superior tone. "Yes I do!" Emma shouted. They both looked around, they were creating a scene. "I think Hitler is the Anti-Christ" she said, lightly. "Oh Emma, you are so wrong" he said. "This world can become a much better place" he continued. "It will be.... when Jesus Christ comes back as King of Kings and Lord of Lords" she countered.

Otto shook his head and smiled "You are so religious" he said. "You are also religious" she snapped back."What are you talking about?" he snarled "I believe in God. You believe in mankind. Mankind only fails" she stated. "Emma you and I are Aryan, We're a master race" he boasted. "All have sinned and come short of the glory of God" she responded "Mankind verses a make believe God, it's always been that way" Otto said. "And there's always been a war" she stated. Otto shrugged and laughed. "A war between Ego-maniacs thinking they can saved the world by making everyone their slaves and Jesus Christ who's going to return to the earth for a final judgment" she shouted. "You and people like you is the reason the world is like it is" Otto shot back. Emma stood up and left the cafe.

Chapter 23

The Eatons loved Los Alamos. Los Angeles was too big and too busy. It was so unlike tiny little Madison Indiana. Los Alamos more of their *cup of tea*. They loved the fact that they were surrounded by so much natural beauty. It was so easy for Doug, Rita and George to spend an entire day, hiking and absorbing all that nature had to give. One weekend they spent the entire time back-packing and sleeping in pup tents. They visited *Bandelier* and spent hours climbing through the old Pueblo Indian cliff dwellings. They were like children at a carnival

After their fireside supper was finished they relaxed by fire and talked things over. Small things had creeped into their living arrangement, like clothes on the floor and the toilet seat not being placed back down. After all the issues came out and the compromises made, the conversation turned to their work. Doug was having a very hard time working with the military and the civilians and keeping their differences at a minimal. "It is hard enough-coordinating all that was going on" he said. "I do not need to be putting up with all of the bickering between the military and the civilians" he said

Rita was teaching second grade and the Civil war was being reenacted. The boys from the south who spoke with a Southern accent and the boys from the northeast with the way they spoke, were constantly fighting one another. Rita had to brake up a fight daily between the Yankees and the Rebels. It was getting way out of hand.

George was troubled but he wasn't talking about it. Rita could see the trouble on his face. After the Sun went down and the stars came out, Doug turned in early. There was a moment of silence but it was soon interrupted by Rita. "Whats eating you, George?" she asked. "Oh, it's not really important" he said. "I know better!" Rita told him.

"Okay, it's like this...We are calculating how powerful we should make the bomb" he said. "And?" was Rita's one word question. "Rita...could make a bomb so powerful, it could destroy the entire world..." he asked. Rita was surprised. "Well we have to build a bomb. What if the Nazis build one and we don't have one to defend ourselves?" she said. "I know all of that! But where does it end?" he said. "They will just build one more powerful than ours and we'll turn around and build one more powerful than that one. And it's going to go on and on till we will both have dooms-day bombs" he continued. She seen his point.

"George, you believe in the Bible, don't you?" she asked. "You know I do" he answered. "What does it say about the second coming of Christ?" she asked. "I see your point...But Rita...it's so scary" he said. "How strong is your faith?" she asked. "I need to do some praying, because I want to quit work and go home" George said. "Your country needs you George... I'll pray for you" Rita told him.

Chapter 24

Emma decided she needed a weapon and with the way   security was at the base getting one would be next to impossible. She remained friendly with Otto, they didn't let their disagreement separate them. She told him that she wanted to learn about firearms because if the base was attacked she wanted to be able to defend herself even though the attackers might be Americans.

Otto took her to the firing range inside the complex and they checked out two German Luger handguns from the arsenal. Otto explained to her everything he knew about the pistol including it's history and how it was developed. Otto had her stuff cotton balls in her ears. He told her to use both of her hands and hold the weapon in front of her, aim at the target and slowly press the trigger.

After she emptied the magazine, he showed her how to remove it and load it with new bullets. She was afraid of the firearm at the start but the more she fired it, her fear went away. Before they finished for the day she fell in love with firing the Luger. Otto showed her how to clean the pistol saying "It needs to be cleaned every time it is used." They returned the weapons to the attendant at the counter of the arsenal and he put both of them on a shelf below. Emma saw what he did and logged it in her mind.

*****

The scientist couldn't come up with an engine powerful enough to control the Haunebu. The craft would rise up off it's platform but afterwards there was no controlling it. They needed a more powerful engine. Maria and Emma was told, they were brought to the secret base to communicate with the aliens on planet Aldeberan to get a design for a more powerful engine.

Maria and Emma joined forces and they both tried to contact them but it was useless. Maria said she needed her four female friends to join her to contact the aliens. Within forty eight hours the four women were at Nazi Ice base 211. After a good night rest, there was a very nice reception for the ladies the next evening, Traute Blohm, Sigrun Kuenheim, Gudrun Jentzsch, and Heike Erhartdt were honored guess at the fancy dinner.

Afterwards it was time to get busy. Maria and her friends went to the conference room which had all of it's furniture removed. Directly across from the conference room was the firing range and arsenal. High in the wall of the conference room was a window that looked into the second floor of the arsenal.

Emma went with the women but she said she needed to use the rest room before she went inside. The ladies went into the conference room and striped down to their underwear. Up behind the second floor window of the arsenal was the attendant having a full view of the women across the passageway taking their clothes off. Emma went to the counter and saw that the attendant wasn't there. She knew where he was at and now was her chance to steal a gun. She checked the door beside her and it was unlocked. She quietly went inside, walked behind the counter and looked under it. Lucky for Emma there was one German Luger on the self. She checked the magazine and it was fully loaded. She picked the gun up exited the room and slowly shut the door

Emma went to the bathroom and took her clothes off. She placed the German Luger on top of her clothes and rolled it all up into a neat little loaf. She walked out of the restroom and down the passageway in her underwear. The attendant was behind the counter and when Emma walked by she cussed at him in German *"Dreh deinen Kopt, pervers"* "Turn your head, pervert." She entered the conference room and joined the five women in a seance.

Maria told the women, the number six has something significant about it and since there was six members in the séance, there should be plenty of power in the room. Emma joined in the chant the women were saying. It was a sentence spoken in Ancient Sumeria. Emma had no idea what she was saying but she went along. They began to chant faster and Emma could feel a heavy presence come over her.

Maria went into a trance and began automatic writing. The presence grew stronger on Emma and finally she fell into a trance. She drifted back to where her last vision stopped. She was being carried by the four young Aryan men to the ancient temple on Aldebaran. They carried her up the steps and two servants opened the two doors leading inside. Just inside the temple was a giant idol. It was a huge Bull with wings and it's eyes began to glow a bright red color. Then two beams of red light came from the Bulls eyes and struck Emma low in her stomach.

She became stiff again and laid down flat as the four men carried her closer to the idol. Then they lifted her up as high as they could reach. Emma started getting a feeling of euphoria, It was ten times stronger than how marijuana made her feel. The intoxication was so strong her body started to tingle all over. The four men who were lifting her began the same chant the women were saying back at the conference room. The citizens behind them began to chant the same words the four men were saying.

Suddenly Emma felt an outside force come over her. She had the feeling of being in the presence of her twin brother. It was the feeling she got when they were both together enjoying themselves as small children. Emma and Ernst were so close to one another, some people thought it was unusual. Sometimes when one of them got hurt, both of them could feel the pain. Once Ernst stepped on broken glass while wading in a creek by their home. Emma also had the same pain. They both cried sitting on the bank of the creek. Neither one of them could walk, finally someone came along and found them. It was so strange to him because Emma didn't even have a scratch on her foot.

Emma got an image of Ernst in her mind. Ernst looked happy and he was doing what he was meant to do, at least that's how the image made Emma feel. Then Emma saw another image. In this image Ernst and George Matthews were busy on a project together. This project was very important, it was like the fate of all of mankind depended on her brother and George. Then words entered in to her mind, it was like she was hearing a voice. "They need you! Their success won't happen without you!"

Emma black-out and woke up in the séance. Aunt Maria was finishing her automatic writing and Sigran began translating the ancient Sumerian into German. Two hours later the Nazis had a new design for an Anti-gravity engine, a "Die Glocke" they called it "The Bell"

Chapter 25

Ernst seemed to fall into a reverie, he couldn't stay concentrated on his work. George noticed it and was afraid he was going to be reprimand. At lunch, he finally got the nerve to ask his friend, "what's bugging you, Ernst?" he asked. "You haven't been your self for days" he went on. Ernst looked up with big sad eyes "it's Emma, I can't stop thinking about her" he said. George put his hand on his friends shoulder "Still, no one has heard a thing from her since she left for Germany with Aunt Maria. If only we knew what city she's living in. That alone would be something" Ernst lamented. He planted his face in his hands for a minute then looked up again "And all the bombing the Allies are doing, I'm afraid she may get killed" he continued. George put his hand on his friends shoulder and said "The best thing we can do is pray" Ernst looked at his friend with a smile and answered "I've been doing plenty of that." George responded with a smile, himself.

They continued meal for a few moments and Ernst started another conversation. "George, Emma and I are very close. I guess it's because we are twins but we share feelings together. What I'm saying is, I can feel her pain and she can feel mine. It's the same with happiness, with fear and sometimes with laughter." George looked at Ernst with unbelief. "That's really something" he said.

Ernst looked George in the eyes with a very serious expression. "I need to share this with you, I need to get something off of my heart" he said. "You can trust me. I will keep it a secret. No one else will know a thing" George answered. "It's about Emma. Last night I had a dream, It was so strange George, there was no images in the dream only feelings..." then he froze. George looked at him and nodded. "...like I said I couldn't see a thing but I knew Emma was about to be raped by the devil or one of the fallen ones" Ernst stopped to get his breathe, then he continued "I just screamed 'No!' and it stopped, it let Emma alone. Then I saw an image, it was a giant bull but he turned and ran away from me" he finished.

George looked at his friend and shook his head. "Do you think God is giving you a message?" he asked his friend. "I think the dream was from God but it was so strange. Also I felt like I was in the same room with Emma. I could feel her presence. It's only a feeling that her and I share together, George." George shrugged.

Chapter 26

Emma hid the German Luger deep in her underwear drawer, with plenty of things stacked over it. The pistol gave her a feeling of power. It was like an equalizer, the most burly man on the base was no more powerful than her as long as she had a weapon.

The new *Die Glocke* Anti-gravity engine was placed in the *Haunebu II* flying saucer and tested only a week after Maria received the new plan. The testing was filmed and that night everyone at the base was able to see the film at the cinema. The freezing temperature made it impossible for any one to witness it outside. Only a few members of the crew were outside when the testing took place. After the completion of the film the entire audience cheered the success of new Nazi flying weapon.

Maria and Emma were at the showing and they both were caught up into all of the excitement. Emma had mixed feeling about the event. The Nazis were her enemies but she couldn't deny that what she witnessed was a great accomplishment.

Instantly after the film, General Hans Kammler walked out on to the stage. The audience stood on their feet and cheered him and the applause went on for over a minute. The General had to do a hand sign for the crowd to stop so he could speak. He went on about what a great night it was for the Nazis. He mentioned all the effort that the different teams had done and he shared the applause with them.

Next he brought out the test pilot for the aircraft Lt. Otto Shoenheit. The cheer for him was more powerful than what the General received. He was very hansom in his full dress uniform. Three teenage girls sitting in the front row cheered and screamed as he waved at the crowd. They through roses on the stage for him. Emma thought they were acting foolish, They were really making a spectacle of themselves. It upset her to the point to where she wanted to get out of her seat and go back to her room.

Emma rose to her feet and her Aunt Maria asked her "Where are you going?" Emma didn't want to tell her the truth. She didn't want to tell her how the silly girls were upsetting her. "I'm thirsty...but I guess I can wait" she said off the top of her head. "I should say so, history is being made" she said. Emma sat back down in her seat and the girls in the front, when an older lady walked next to them and gave them a disapproving look.

Emma and Maria were finishing their popcorn and soda pop when Otto came along and said "hello" to them. Maria congratulated him for being chosen for the test pilot position. "Without you, there would be no *Haunebu* flying craft. It was you who got the design for it engine" he told her. Thank you for receiving the information from the *Aldebarans*" he continued.

"What did you think about the film" he asked Emma. "I wish the *Haunebu* wasn't a war machine" she answered. "I completely understand your feelings and I'm very sympathetic. "Many American lives will be lost because of our advanced technology, the technology that went into building this aircraft, but maybe the *Haunebu* will bring a quick end to this awful war" he said.

Emma didn't want to argue with him. He was an arrogant Nazi officer and an argument would lead no where. "Would you like to see the inside of the *Haunebu?*" he asked her. "If we get caught, you'll get in trouble" she told him. "We won't get caught and even if we did , it would be worth cheering up a pretty girl like you"

Now was Emma chance, the time she has been waiting for to escape this Nazi prison. Otto was flirting with her and she was going to take full advantage of it. "Otto, let me change out of this dress into some slacks and I will meet you at the hanger in a few minutes.

Emma hid the Luger pistol in her back waist line. The top she choose to wear was long and covered her back perfectly. Once inside the craft Emma started acting starry eyed and flirty. Otto ate it up, explaining things to her was exciting to him. "What does this lever do? How do you steer the craft? How do you make it rise? How do you start the engine? How fast will it go?" she bombarded him with questions that he answered with a huge smile on his face. She acted as stupid as a box of rocks but she was taking notes in his mind.

"So you fly this craft with these two "Joy-sticks?" she asked taking them in her hands. "Yes, You push them forward and the craft goes down. Pull them to you and the craft goes up. Pull them both to the right and the craft goes right. Pull them to the left and it goes left and at your right foot is the accelerator" he explained.

Being a college girl, Emma knew what his next move was going to be. Ernst came up behind her and put his arms around her. He put his hands over her hands to show her how to fly the machine. Emma did an about face and gave him a sexy stare. He smiled and hugged tighter, then she reached for the Luger in her back belt line. When Otto was about to give her a kiss, Emma whipped out the Lugar and pointed it inches from his nose. "Dummkopf zuruckziehen!" (back off dumb head) she said in German. Otto's heart fell to his feet. The cat backed the mouse into a corner.

Emma pressed the button on the console and the overhead doors of the roof began to open. Alarms and red lights flash in the hanger bay and guards came running forward but they couldn't do a thing. One of the guards was foolish enough to take a shot at the craft. It bounced off without scratching the paint. Next Emma started the engine and pulled both of the joysticks forward and the craft rose. Otto lunged at her but she turned and shot him in the knee cap and was back flying the craft before it lowered an inch. He decided, then to behave himself and except being a prisoner.

"I know any direction I fly is going to be north. I want to know have to find. 118.24 W latitude?" she demanded to know. Otto stayed silent. "I just blew your knee cap off, if you don't tell me how to find it, I'll blow the other one off." she yelled. "You're not taking me to the United States" he yelled back. "If you don't want to crash in the ocean or end up in some third world country in South America, you'll show me how to fly home" she said, a little softer this time.

"Once we are a hundred miles from here, we will be able to get a better barring of where we are at. There's no way of knowing exactly where we are at unless we contact the people you just left." Otto said. Emma looked at him with disgust and didn't say a word. It sounded to Emma like he was co-operating so she flew in a forward direction. "Just get me to the States, that all I ask" she said.

Two hours later, Otto had Emma descend so they could see the land beneath them. They saw a group of lights and headed for them and once they got there, they continued to fly north. In a few minutes they saw another group of lights. "These are port towns below us. Fly down where we can see them" Otto said and Emma did as he said. They flew low enough to see that it was a seaport town. "Fly to the right and go over land" he said. Emma obeyed. Soon they came onto another coast line. "We're in Panama" he said. "Lets remain flying low until we see the canal" he said. Once they saw the lights of canal, Emma pulled the joy-sticks back and climbed out of sight from the ground.

Chapter 27

Ernst met George at their breakfast table and he looked like he just won the Irish sweepstakes. "What has gotten into you, this morning?" George asked looking up at him, digging through his scrambled eggs, afraid to take a bite. "George, it's Emma, I feel like I'm going to see her soon" he said. George could only give his friend a blank look. "I know, it sounds so crazy, George, but this feeling is so strong." he said.

"Ernst, I don't want to pop your balloon but do you know what you are saying?" He seriously looked at Ernst. "Emma is in Germany, we are at war with Germany. "We're living in a top secret military insulation. No one outside of here knows where you are at. How can Emma go from Germany to the United States with this war going on? I know with the faith of a mustard see, you can move mountains. Ernst, what you're saying is like moving a mountain."

"George, I've been telling myself that since I woke up this morning" he said. "But this feeling is so strong, I can't shake it off." Again, George only gave his friend a blank look. "Ernst, I'm sorry but I just don't have that kind of faith. I pray this war we end soon and Emma comes home alive...That's all the faith I have" George told his friend. Ernst shook his head "Yes" and smiled. "All we can do now is wait and see what happens" he said. Then Ernst looked at the scrambled eggs on his plate and his smile went away.

George and Ernst left the dining hall and were on their way to the building they work at, when Tony Shrum came riding up to them on a new motorcycle. He came to a complete stop, put the bike in neutral and revved the engine. Then he turned the engine off and removed his sunglasses and smiled. "This bike kicks butt!" he said. "What is it?" Ernst asked looking the motorcycle over. "It's a special desert bike Harley Davidson built for the Army. It called an XA750, man, this beauty will fly!" he bragged. "Have you rode it at top speed?" George asked him. "I have to have some asphalt under me to do that" he answered. "I just took a ride out in the desert and boy, does this thing handle great!"

Before Tony started the motorcycle to leave, he told his two friends "There two more of these for sale at the motor pool" George and Ernst did an about face and looked at Tony. "The army decided to only to build the *Jeep*, said they really didn't need motorcycles, boy, that was stupid. This bike will run rings around a *Jeep*" Tony told them. "They have two more of these for sale, you say?" Ernst asked. "I almost stole the thing, the bike is worth a lot more than what I paid for it and they're selling it to me on time" Tony said. George and Ernst looked at one another and they both shook their heads "Yes." "Tony, tell Dr. Oppenheimer we will be at work as soon as we buy those two motorcycles" Ernst asked. "He won't mind" Tony replied.

That weekend the three guys rode their bikes a short distance to the hilly terrain outside the project. The three of them decided they wanted to be experts in handling their motorcycles on the hilly terrain going as fast as they could. All three of them, at least once, took a dive from their bikes into the soft sand. They learned the hard way. But they discovered how fast they could take a turn or go over a hill. Tony explained to his two friends how to race over a hill. First, you slow down, just a little, then right before you reach the peck of the hill, you give the bike, full throttle. You will be on your back wheel only and you will go airborne at the top of the hill. But when you land, it will be on the back wheel. Never land on the front wheel, you're sure to crash if that happens. Tony said they must have three Angels watching over them, too many times they should have crashed but they didn't.

A week later the three of them held a *Hare & Hound* type race. The race coarse went from El Rancho cross country to Los dos. It was a ten mile race across the hilly topography. There was no rules to the race.

The race started with the firing of a pistol and ended with the winner pulling the yellow pennant out of the ground. Kitty Oppenheimer was the official at the start. She was the one to fire the pistol and she was there to see that no one "Jumped the gun."

Dr. Oppenheimer was on the other end of the coarse to see the fellow who pulled up the pennant didn't get it taken away from him by a sore loser. The three racers were best of friends but sometimes competition brings out the worst in people.

The morning of the race brought two spectators to the race coarse. Kitty at the starting line and Dr. Oppenheimer at the finish. The boys started their engines. There is just something about the sound of three Harley Davidson motorcycles beside each other being revved up by their riders. Kitty really didn't like the roar they made. She said it sounded like an army of tuba horns coming to kill you. Dr. Oppenheimer loved the sound they made. He said it sounded like American warriors on two wheels.

When the shot gun was fired, the race began. Tony jumped out front but Ernst wasn't far behind. George followed close behind Ernst. George was the careful type of guy, he really didn't mind being the last to finish as long as he could stay close to the other two. But it wasn't that way with Tony and Ernst, it was a neck to neck race for the entire ten miles.

After about eight mile into the race the two riders were racing full throttle next to one another. It was like the two motorcycles were acting in unison with each other. Ernst's bike was headed toward a huge sage brush in front of him. He had no other choice but to serve to avoid it and when he did he lost his advantage and fell behind making Tony the leader. Before Ernst was able to get straightened out George was racing next to him. That didn't last for long.

George could tell that Ernst was angry at what happen. It made him so mad he started riding like a wild man. He rode over a hill and as he was flying through the air he push down with his feet on the foot pegs while he jerked up on the handle bars. This kept his front wheel higher than the back. He was airborne much longer than George had ever seen anyone go. He went much higher and went much longer in mid air than what George thought was possible.

Ernst's motorcycle kept going faster and faster as he went. The bike was acting more like a high-spirited race horse instead of a piece of machinery. Ernst went over two more hills and with each one of them, he flew higher and traveled longer in the air. Finally Ernst pasted Tony on the left and took away his lead. Tony was shocked but he couldn't get any more speed from his Harley Davidson. Ernst got a big lead on Tony with just a quarter mine to the pennant. A huge hill was in front of him but he did not slow down at all. The bike kept going faster and faster and as he reached it's peak Ernst did what he had to do to make it land on the back wheel. When the motorcycle landed, it was on it back wheel but Ernst got too high and was going too fast. He came down hard and wasn't able to keep from crashing. Ernst was ten feet from his motorcycle when Tony pulled next to him. He laid there still as a statue.

George rode up and seen what had happened "I'm going to get Dr. Oppenheimer!" he shouted and rode away. Dr. Oppenheimer seen the accident through his binoculars and was already driving to the scene in his station wagon when George rode up. They loaded Ernst into the vehicle and rushed him to sick bay at the base.

Chapter 28

As Emma continued flying north she began to tire. Otto was laying down asleep on the deck behind her, not making a sound. Earlier he managed to make himself a bandage for his wound from the shirt he was wearing. He stopped bleeding a half hour after she shot him so he wasn't in any kind of danger of bleeding to death.

The thought of shooting someone started to trouble her mind. *"I can't believe how easily I shot him"* Emma thought to herself. *"What if I killed him. Could I live with myself if I did that?"* she reasoned. It was now twenty four hours that Emma had been awake. The need to sleep was growing stronger for her. She caught herself falling asleep so she got out of her chair and stood to fly the craft. She discovered if she pushed the two thumb buttons at the same time on the joy-sticks. The craft would fly with automatic pilot. Now she was free to go through all the stuff that was stored away in the compartments under the console. Emma found a pill bottle, it read *Pillen aufwecken.* (awake pills). Emma poured two of them in her hand, then popped them in her mouth. She washed them down with water from a canteen hanging on the wall.

Fifteen minutes later Emma was wide awake but she was intoxicated from the stimulants she took. She began to feel dizzy like the aircraft was spinning the way a merry-go-round would be. Then the same feeling came over her that she had of the vision on *Aldebaran*. She didn't see any visions but the feeling she got was strong. Emma sat in her chair and sleepiness set in again. Her mind flash back to *Aldebaran* and the giant bull she was being sacrificed to. Then she was tackle and fell on the floor. She managed to turn over and Otto was on top of her. He put both of his hands on her throat and began to strangle her. She still had the Luger in her hand and she fired it into the side of his body. He screamed in agony and walked as far as he could away from her. He slid down the till he was sitting down and tears of fear streamed down his face

All of a sudden, on it's own, the craft stopped and started descending. "We're running out of fuel I hope we're not over water" Otto yelled. "What's happening" Emma demanded him to tell her. "The craft was programmed to land on it's own when the fuel is low" he answered. Emma looked out the porthole window and it looked like they were above a desert terrain. A blast of thrust beneath the craft fired for a brief moment to slow it down from landing too fast and crashing.

The *Haunebu* made a perfect landing, like it was programmed to do but waiting for it's arrival was a dozen military jeeps loaded with soldiers. Emma prayed, the landing was in the United States. She opened up the exit hatch and Otto shouted "Where are you going?" She shouted back without turning around "Home, I hope!"

Emma descended down the ladder and someone standing in front of his jeep yelled "Freeze!" She put her feet onto terra firma and did a slow about face, placing her hands in the air, all at the same time. *"Sprichst du Englisch?"* (Do you speak English?) The officer yelled again.

"I'm American" she answered with a perfect Minnesota accent. "Your aircraft has *swastikas* painted all over it. "The Nazi pilot is inside badly wounded" she answered. "Go check it out, corporal" the lieutenant ordered. The soldier lowered his rifle and said "But sir, we don't know what that thing is" The lieutenant sharply answered "You have been ordered...Go do your job"

Emma interrupted "You'll be okay, he's unarmed and badly wounded" she told the warrior. The corporal handed his rifle over to the soldier standing next to him and took out the 45 caliber, he carried on his side. Very cautiously he made his way into the *Haunebu*. "Are you armed.

Miss?" the lieutenant asked her. "Yes, I have a German Luger" she answered. "Remove it slowly and throw it on the ground." he demanded. She did as he requested.

The officer removed a pair of handcuffs from a small holster attached to his belt. "Keep an eye on her, private, if she makes a move, shoot her" he ordered. As he approached her, Emma broke into tears. She was tire and sleepy. She had been through so much, she couldn't take it any more. She through her arms around the lieutenant and fell limp. The officer hugged her enough to keep her on her feet. "I have been through so much lately, you have no idea how happy I am to be back home and in the presence of the US Army." she cried.

The lieutenant scooped her up in his arms and carried her to his jeep. He put her in the passenger seat next to where he was driving. "Get that kraut out of that contraption, put his sorry hide in the ambulance and let's get the hell out of here" Then he ordered two of the soldiers to stay there and guard the foo-fighter. Before everyone drove away the lieutenant spoke "Listen up! No one speak a word about this incident. No one is to know about this flying craft. Consider it "top secret" punishable by dead if word leaks out...Is there any questions?" No one said a word "Move out!" the lieutenant shouted and everyone drove away.

Chapter 29

The army doctor thoroughly examined Ernst and found a severely cracked femur bone on his right side and three broken ribs. He had to be hospitalize for a week which he didn't think was necessary but the doctor didn't agree. The doctor also gave Ernst and his two pals a major chewing out when he found the three of them together. "Sports is sports, I understand all of that. But you should play as safe as you can." he said firmly. "And none of you were wearing helmets, right?" The three of them only looked at one another. "How about a turn off switch in case you get thrown from the bike?" he said. "What if Ernst's bike kept on going and it ran over him at 60mph?"

Thankfully, they did consider everything the doctor said. Tony talked to his friends at the motor pool and they rigged up a kill-switch for all three motorcycles. Kitty bought the three boys crash helmets from the motorcycle store in Santa Fe. All three of them wanted helmets and she made sure they had them.

*****

May 8th 1945 V.E. Day. Germany surrenders to the Soviet Union and the allies in Europe. The war is over in that part of the world. The entire free world celebrates their victory. Cities across the country have parades and dancing in the street. Streets are littered with ticker-tape. Children wave miniature US flags, everyone was grateful because our boys were coming home.

Things were a bit different at Los Alamos. The atom bomb, the reason for the entire project, was now, not necessary. The scheduled testing of the bomb was just a few weeks away. Feelings were mixed in the community, most of the civilian population wanted to stop the develop and go back home. Most of the military didn't want to change a thing. They wanted to move forward and complete making the Bomb.

Debates happened every where at the facility. How big a threat is the Soviet Union? Should we drop the bomb on the Japanese? Should the bomb be develop only to have it in our arsenal, regardless of a threat. Everyone at Los Alamos had a strong opinions about the matter. Hardly a soul was in the middle of the road with their point of view.

On Saturday night a fight broken out between a soldier and a civilian. There was a dance at Theater "Two" and some how, alcohol found it's way into the crowd. The two men were debating about the bomb when the fight broke out. The incident showed Doctor Oppenheimer and General Groves how much of a tinderbox the situation was. They decided to have a temporary shut down until the government made a decision about the bomb.

The government decided to keep developing the bomb but they hadn't made up their minds about using it on the Japanese. On July 16th 1945 the first atomic weapon test was conducted near Alamogordo, New Mexico. It was code named "Trinity." It took place early that morning before the sun came up. Trinity was drop from a 200 foot tower. The bomb exploded and the night sky became like a noon day sun.

Later that day, Doctor Oppenheimer's reaction of watching the explosion was filmed. "We know the world would not be the same... A few people laughed, a few people cried, most people were silent....I remembered the line from the Hindu scripture, the Bhagavad Gita; Vishnu is trying to persuade the Prince that he should do his duty and, to impress him, takes on his multi-armed form and says, 'Now I am become Death, the destroyer of worlds"

Chapter 30

Just outside of Roswell New Mexico is where Emma landed in the Nazi aircraft. She was taken to the infirmary at the army air base, along with Otto. He was taken to one side of the building and she was on the opposite side. They both had guards posted outside their doors, just to be careful. Otto's wounds were serious but not life threatening. The army doctors were able to treat him before matters became worst.

The Army didn't want the public to know about a strange Nazi flying machine landing in New Mexico so it became a Top Secret. Emma was integrated and they checked to make sure there was a missing Emma Orsic from Milwaukee. Emma wanted to go home so badly but she understood the nature of her predicament. She co-operated with the military and what they had to do. The government did let Emma's parents know that she was in the United States and she was alive and very healthy. But they had to keep her under detention because of the circumstances of her return to the US.

Emma was put in the watch of a young female corporal named Anesthesia Brown from Decatur Illinois. She was Emma age and a Military Policeman in for the army. Anesthesia could not let Emma out of her sight, not even for a second. Going to the bathroom was Emma's only break. Anesthesia and her subject got along very well. Emma rode along with Anesthesia as she patrolled the base in a jeep. The army gave Emma uniforms to wear to make it look the two were partners. They both were very pretty and the young male soldiers turned their heads as they drove by. They quickly became the talk of the army base among the young soldiers. Once a soldier asked "what would it take for me to get arrested. The trouble I'd get into would be worth the ride you two would give me." It was just the kind of thing the girls heard all the time.

After two weeks of being in Roswell, Emma had a dream and Ernst was in it. Ernst was driving their Dad's Stutz Bearcat with the top down. She was riding with him. It was a picture perfect day and it warmed Emma's heart to be with her brother again. The area they were driving in looked like New Mexico. It was a two lane blacktop highway in the desert with mountains in the background.

Emma woke up from the dream with the feeling that her brother was not far away. *How can he be close she thought to herself? He may be in prison some where in Wisconsin.* She was not allowed to talk to any friends or relatives from back home. But the feeling that Ernst was near was very strong and the feeling would not go away. He was on her mind all the time. All she could do was pray for him.

*****

Anesthesia's evaluation report came back and she got the highest recommendations available. Because of her achievements, she received a weekend pass. It was great news for her but it upset Emma. "Who's going to guard me this weekend? Some old wicked witch of the west?" she asked. Anesthesia didn't answer but looked away. Soon she answered "No, your fairy god-mother is guarding you this weekend" Emma put on a sour face "Oh come on, Anesthesia. That's not funny!" she said. "No Emma.....your coming with me. We're going to Albuquerque, no arguments. I'm from the big city and I need some civilization" she said.

Emma was shocked "did I hear you right? I can go with you?" she asked. "Since you've been here, you have totally co-operated. You've obeyed all the rules, you've pulled your own load. If you were a soldier your evaluation would be as high as mine" Anesthesia told her. The news brought tears to her eyes "For the longest time I've felt like a prisoner, like a trouble maker and now, you're telling me, the army trusts me?" Emma said. "That's how the army operates. Emma" Anesthesia said. "That's better news than my freedom to go with you" Emma said.

"I have something to show you" Anesthesia told Emma as the walked to the *chow hall.* "The commander of the base asked me where I was going. When I told him, Albuquerque, he said that I would need a way to get there..." she explained but Emma interrupted her. "He going to let us borrow a jeep?" she asked. Anesthesia stopped and faced her friend "No....it's better than that" she said. "What do you mean, Anesthesia?" Emma asked. "Look behind me. What do you see?" she said. "What?" Emma reacted. "What do you see, parked behind me?" Anesthesia asked. "Okay Anesthesia, it's a 1936 Stutz Bearcat, my dad has one just like it" Emma answered. "This car belongs to the commander!" she said. Emma's jaw dropped "Are you saying, this is what we'll be driving?" She instantly thought about her dream

Chapter 31

The government decided to use the Atom bomb on Japan. Our military forces was pushing Japan back but it was a slow process and costing too many lives. The estimate was, the quickest end to the Pacific front would take a year and cost thousands of lives. Japan said the only way the war would end would be to kill the last man standing. Dropping the bomb would also be the humane way of treating the Japanese, our military leaders said. Developing a bomb to be dropped from a B-29 aircraft was done at Los Alamos. Personal was working around the clock to get the job done. Ernst and George put in 16 hour days for over a week.

Their week schedule was grueling. All they were doing was eating drinking sleeping and working. Ernst had a very difficult time falling asleep at night. Too often, he would have a dream of being with Emma. One night he had the same dream that his sister had. He was driving with her in their Dad's Stutz Bearcat through a desert in New Mexico. When he woke he was overcoming with the greatest affection for her. He couldn't go back to sleep. He tossed and turned for the rest of the night.

The next day was a Friday and that afternoon everyone was busy. Doctor Oppenheimer walked to where the boys were working and found Ernst asleep in his chair, in front of his desk. George was beside him, fixed in a daze, staring at a slide rule. He had no idea that his partner was asleep. The doctor knew the two of them have been over worked. He woke Ernst and told him and George to take the weekend off.

Ernst had a dream where George and him rode their motorcycles to Albuquerque. Nothing about the dream was unusual but the dream was very vivid. The sounds, the smells, the sights all felt so real in his dream, riding his bike through the city. When Ernst woke up the next morning he told George about the dream and said "We must go there" he said. George agreed because he really didn't care where he went as long as he could go there on his Harley.

The trip to Albuquerque didn't take as long as they thought it would. The traffic was light and the boys rode well over the speed limit. There was plenty of long straight stretches through the desert and the boys could open up the throttle and *let'er rip*. They entered Albuquerque city limits around noon and the streets were busy with shopping and other business. Stopped at a traffic light, Ernst saw a car drive in front of them. "George! That car looked just like my Dad's Bearcat" he yelled over at his friend The light turned green and Ernst turned right and rocketed down the city street. George had a hard time keeping up with his partner but he managed. Ernst's rode so fast it became dangerous. He weaved from lane to lane, passing cars, trying to catch the Bearcat. George signaled for him to slow down but he wouldn't. They rode past a parked police car and George said to himself "We're in trouble now." The police car did not move, "guess he didn't see us" George thought.

Ernst caught up to the car and pulled over behind Anesthesia and Emma. Ernst didn't recognize Emma and he could only get a glimpse of Anesthesia, who was driving. Emma didn't recognize her brother because he was wearing a helmet and sun glasses. George pulled beside Ernst and they both followed the girls in the car. George thought Ernst was loosing his mind and signaled him to let the girls go. Anesthesia was panicked but Emma wasn't. The entire ordeal puzzled her emotions. "Pull over" Emma said to Anesthesia. "Are you nuts!" she responded. "I can't explain it but we must pull over" Emma demanded. "But those two bikers are following us" Anesthesia objected. "I don't care, just do it" Emma yelled.

Anesthesia pulled into the parking lot of a crowded supermarket and Ernst followed her. George stayed back a few yards, he didn't want any part of this. Ernst parked his bike and walk closer to the Bearcat "what do you want?" Anesthesia yelled at him. Then he noticed his sister. He froze, he couldn't say a word. Emma still didn't recognize him. "Emma" he said. Anesthesia looked over at Emma. "Do you know that guy?" she asked. Emma couldn't say a word but tears roll down her cheeks. Ernst took off his helmet and sun glasses and Emma saw who he was. "ERNST!" she shouted. She jumped out of the Bearcat without opening the passenger door. She through her arms around her brother so hard it about knocked him over.

She cried joyful tears and kept repeating his name. Ernst's eyes began to water "I can't believe this. How could this be happening?" he said. Then George walked up to see what was going on and Emma recognized him. "George?" she asked. George saw who it was and his jaw dropped. "I thought you were in Germany" he said. Emma ran over and hugged George as hard as she did her brother. "Could someone, please tell me what is going on?" Anesthesia asked. "This is my twin brother and a friend" Emma told her. "The brother you thought was in jail?" she asked. Emma didn't know what to say. "We didn't go to jail, Emma" he told his sister. "We have a lot of catching up to do" she told her brother.

Chapter 32

The four of them walked along Central ave, window shopping as they went. Ernst held his sister's hand for a few minutes until she said "Ernst, we aren't children anymore" Ernst blushed "I guess, I just don't want to loss you again" he explained. "I want to buy some *cowgirl boots*" Anesthesia said as they walked by a western wear store. "I think I'd like a pair, also" Emma said. The guys looked at one another and George said "It would be good for riding our bikes" Ernst didn't say a work but directed every one into the store.

It didn't take long for the four of them to split apart once they were inside the store. The girls went one way and the boys another. Anesthesia walked to the back corner of the store with Emma. "Your brother is so cute!" she told her friend. Emma only smiled. The exact same thing happened with the guys. "Anesthesia, sure is a knock-out!" Ernst said to George. He agreed but he wanted to say that Emma was twice as pretty as she was three years ago. How could he? Ernst was her brother, her protector, how could he say any thing like that to him? George respected Emma but saying she was pretty to her brother could end up in a fight.

After a short while, all four of them wandered apart from one another. No one was able to find the correct pair of western boots. Anesthesia stood in front of a small floor mirror modeling a pair of boots when Ernst walked by "What do you think of these?" she asked him. "Those look great on you!" he said with a smile. From then on it was nothing but smiles and talk. George saw the two of them and froze in his tracks to watch. *Ernst is so smooth with the girls. How does he do it? Is it his smile? Is it what he says? I just don't understand?* George stood in the isle of the western wear store, perplexed. Emma walked up beside him and saw what he was spying on before he could hide the fact. "They are perfect for one another" she said to George, not taking her eyes away from the romance.

Both of them watched the sparks fly between the two of the them but Emma interrupted their bird watching. "You've change so much in the last three years, George" she told him. "What?" he said startled. "You looked like a young professor back then but now you look....well....you look like a cowboy" she told him. "Is that a good thing?" he asked without thinking. "Of coarse it's a good thing. Don't be silly" she answered. George blushed, he couldn't say another word. The four of them found the perfect boots to buy. When they left the store Ernst walked with Anesthesia and George walked with Emma. It was like that for the entire weekend. It was like a double date made in heaven.

It was such a strange thing for Ernst and Emma. He couldn't say a thing about the work he was doing at Los Alamos. Emma couldn't say anything about her experience in Germany and the Antarctic. They booth were hiding government secrets from one another. They never hid anything from one another. It felt so wrong to the both of them. On Sunday after noon it was time for them to depart. George got the surprise of his when Emma hugged and kissed him. The girls drove south and the boys rode north.

Chapter 33

When Doctor Oppenheimer heard about the boys' weekend in Albuquerque he became perturbed. Ernst told him how amazing it was to run into her there but she could not tell him anything about the last three years of her life. *What happened to Ernst's sister? Why was the government keeping three years of her life a secret?* He thought it was a violation of her rights as a citizen to be served a *gag order* such as that. Finally the Doctor gave General Leslie Groves a phone call (he was the one in charge of the military side of the operations at Los Alamos) "General, what's going on down in Roswell?" he instantly asked. "What did you hear?" the General reluctantly asked. "My assistant's sister has been gagged and sequestered there" he answered. "It's a Top Secret" the General replied. "Oh c'mon

General! Didn't we agree there was to be no secrets between us?" he responded.

"Emma Orsic landed some sort of Nazi foo-fighter directly on the airbase there. She shot the pilot and would have killed him if we didn't get him to the army hospital in time" he told Oppenheimer. "Where did they fly from?" Oppenheimer asked. "Antarctica, she says" the General answered. The conversation went on for a few minutes, the General told him everything he knew about the story. "If it wasn't for the flying saucer, I wouldn't believe a word of it" the General said. "Did you question the pilot" Oppenheimer asked. "The *Kraut* won't say anything about it" the General answered. The European war is over so we can't interrogate him and we have to ship him home as soon as he recovers" the General continued.

Ernst and George were perplexed when Doctor Oppenheimer filled them in on the secrets about Emma. Flying saucers, messages from people on distant planets, a hidden military base at Antarctica, it all sounded so strange to the both of them. Ernst expressed his desire to see his sister again to Doctor Oppenheimer. At the moment he couldn't because of her situation. The Doctor said he would try to get special permission for him to visit her at the base in Roswell. "Doctor could you ask if George could come with me" he asked.

George, Ernst and Tony finished a project before it was due so Oppenheimer gave the boys the afternoon off. They took the moment to enjoy their motorcycles. The three of them rode out to the desert, their favorite place to ride. George rode too close to a cactus and the needles tore through the jeans he was wearing. If it wasn't for his boots the cactus would have done a lot of damage to his leg. "That's why we wear boots out here" he said to George, looking at his torn bluejeans.

The fellows huddled together for a moment to decide where to go next. The sun was going down and there was only around an hour riding time left. George let his two partners know that he wanted to watch the sun set. He suggested the huge hill next to the highway near Cuyamongue. They rode away quickly and got there in about a half hour. They sat on top of the hill facing west drinking from their canteens. A cool breeze started blowing and it felt great to the boys,

The three of them talked shop for about fifteen minutes. Then Ernst shared what was bothering him. "Every bomb we build is bigger than the last one. When is it going to stop?" he said. "Ya' know the

Soviet Union is close to developing an Atom bomb" Tony said. "We might end up in a war with them" George said. They all went silent with that thought. "Do you think we'll, really, drop the bomb on Japan?" Ernst asked, interrupting the silence. "It would finish the war if we did" George answered. "I don't know, we might have to blow that island off the map" Tony said. "We could build a bomb that would be powerful enough to do that" George said. "When is it going to stop?" Ernst asked. The three went silent again. "Ya know something, we could build a bomb so powerful, it could destroy the entire earth" Ernst said. "Mankind is not going to destroy the earth with a bomb" George said. "How can you be so sure?" Ernst asked. "Jesus Christ is coming back to make a new Heaven and Earth" George answered. "Is that what you believe, George?" Ernst asked. "Of coarse I do, it's in the bible" George answered. "How about you, Tony. Is that what you believe?" Ernst asked. Tony looked at George "I don't go to church but I believe in God and if it's in the bible. It must be true" he answered.

"Ya know, I'm thankful for science, we have come a long way in technology in this century alone" George said. "Think about all the new things that has been developed in the last forty years. Automobiles, Airplanes, Radios, Telephones and they introduced, what is know as a Television at the World's Fair. It's like watching a movie with sound but the image is on a picture tube. Think how crazy it would be watching a movie in your living room" George went on. "I saw that in "Science Magazine" but I don't think I'll ever afford to buy one" Ernst commented.

"The point I want to make is, Science is great but lots of it is lies. Like Evolution. Academia calls it science but it's not it's only a theory. They teach it like it's absolutely the truth" George said. "Ya, once I asked a professor during class about creation and he about took my head off. I've never do that again" Tony said. "I believe when the public finds out about the atom bomb, Academia is going to teach it's going bring an end to the planet, Just like you were questioning about earlier, Ernst" George said. "I believe in the Bible so you have to be right, George" Ernst said. "It's like Christianity is in a war with Academia. It truly is a war, a war about forever" George said.

Chapter 34

The news of Roswell had the Pentagon doing cartwheels. "When you have in your custody an actual Nazi fly saucer, you can't wish it would just go away" The secretary of Defense stated in a committee. After a few weeks and lots of round table discussion, the top brass decided to send a secret flotilla to Antarctica. Their mission was to survey and engage the enemy if they should attack. Only Admiral Byrd knew why the flotilla was cruising to the South Pole. Everyone from the Captains down to the Seamen had no idea the purpose of their going there.

While all this was being planned, on August 6th 1945 a B-29 bomber dropped an atom bomb on the city of Hiroshima. With all the devastation, the Japanese still would not surrender their aggression. Three days later a second bomb was dropped on the Japanese city of Nagasaki. The Emperor decided that was enough and surrendered.

On Wednesday August 15th 1945 Japan announced their surrender and word of that surrender was discovered the following afternoon at Los Alamos. The entire base stopped what they were doing and began to celebrate. The operations they accomplished bought an end to the war. All the work at the base stopped and people took to the streets dancing to the jazz music blaring over the PA system. Doctor Oppenheimer allowed George and Ernst to have a four days weekend. They were on their motorcycles within minutes after they got word of their pass.

They reached their destination in Roswell around midnight. And the base was still in the middle of a party and it didn't look like it was going to be over soon. The guys met the girls in the lobby of their barracks where they were waiting for them. Ernst phoned the barracks earlier to let them know they were on their way. Emma and Anesthesia were very happy the war was over but they had no desire to celibate the way everyone else was partying. "I have no interest in drinking tonight" Anesthesia told everyone. "Nor do I" Emma repeated. "The last time I got drunk I was sick for days" she added. It didn't bother the boys one bit, they only wanted to be with the girls. "Let's take a ride on the bikes, let's get away from this mess" Ernst said. "Aren't you tired of riding?" Emma asked. "Not at all. I love it" Ernst said.

Anesthesia climbed on the behind Ernst and Emma behind George and they rode into the night. They traveled west toward Ruidoso, the sky was clear and the stars were many but there was a chill in the air. Emma was wearing slacks and a sweater but she was uncomfortable riding on the bike until she hugged George tightly from behind. They followed behind Ernst and followed him farther as he exited the highway onto a dirt road. Ernst spotted the highest hill on the horizon and rode there. He stopped on the peak of the hill and George rode up next to him and stopped also. The boys killed the engine and it was so peaceful to hear nothing but silence.

The desert below them was lovely, The many stars glittered and the moon was bright. Even tough it was night they could see the entire valley below them. "This is the perfect way to celibate the end of the war" Emma said. Everyone agreed, then she saw her brother put his arm around her best friend. Emma was so happy to see the romance taking place between the two of them. George looked over and noticed the two, also, he looked at Emma with a smile and gave her the thumbs up. Emma returned his smile.

All of a sudden, Emma stood up and looked down the hill. "What do you see, Emma?" George asked. "I don't know" she answered him. Then Ernst rose to his feet. "Do you see it, Ernst?" Emma asked. "No! I feel it" he answered his sister. "I feel it too" she said. Ernst started walking down the hill and Emma followed him. George came next. "You can't come, George, go back!" he told his friend. "What are you saying!" George demand an answer. "Trust me George you can't come with us" Ernst answered. George turned around and went back up to where Anesthesia was at and took a seat next to her. They both watched the brother and sister go to the bottom of the hill and stop.

"They're just standing there. What are they doing?" Anesthesia asked George. "It beats me. Some times I think he just loses his mind" George said. "And she's just like him" Anesthesia remarked. "I can't say for sure but it looks like they are talking but not to each other" George said. "That's what I was thinking" Anesthesia told him. "He is talking to some one, Anesthesia, look at him using his hands" George said. "This is getting scary, George" she reacted. "We need to go back to the base when they are finished down there" George said. As soon as George said, Ernst and Emma stopped their conversation with the *unknown*. They did an about face and started back up the hill. "Let's go" Ernst said when he reached the top.

When they got back to the base, the party was still go on. People were still drinking and dancing. Some of them were past out and laying on the sidewalk. Ernst rode his motorcycle through the base until he came to a hanger. "Is this where it's at?" he asked Emma. "Yes it is" she answered. Ernst walked to the door and the three followed him. The door was unlocked and he walked inside. "So much for security. This place is suppose to be guarded" he said. He turned the lights on and everyone saw a round object covered in canvass. "Help me take this off, George" Ernst said as he removed the covering. George helped him and they both uncover the flying saucer Emma flew in on.

George, Ernst and Anesthesia stood there staring at the flying machine in shock. "Come on, let's roll this thing out of here" Emma yelled at them. She went and opened the huge bay doors and then joined the three pulling the flying saucer out of the hanger. Once they got the craft outside, Anesthesia could take no more "What are we doing?" she yelled. "We talked to a man at the bottom of the hill..." Ernst was saying. "George and I didn't see a man!" she yelled back. "It was an angel, Anesthesia" Emma said. "You two have lost your minds!" She yelled again.

George was troubled at what was going on but he finally spoke up "I believe them, Anesthesia. I know how crazy all of this is but God could have sent one of his Angels here to us to do something important" he said. Anesthesia shook her head "I've come along this far, I may as well finish it" she said and helped them push the craft into position. As Emma carried the ladder to the saucer Ernst approached her "Take me with You" he told his sister. "I can't do that" she said. "There's enough room for me" he came back at her. "That's not it, Ernst" she said as she leaned the ladder against the craft. "Why?" he shouted. "Because I may not come back!" she shouted. "I'll take that risk!" he shouted back. "What if Mom and Dad loss both of us?.....I'm not taking you with me" she reasoned. "How are you going to fly that thing and fire it's weapon at the same time?" Ernst said. "I'll go with her" George said to Ernst. Ernst froze, he couldn't say a word. "Your sister is right, it would be too much for your parents to lose the both of you." he said.

"George, I..." Emma tried to say something but she realize how foolish it would be to go alone. "You need some one to fire the weapon and I'm your man" George said. Emma climbed to the top of the aircraft and sat down beside the hatch. She looked back at George, she wanted to say "No" to him but it would be suicide if she didn't take him along.

"Climb on board" she said as she threw the hatch open and entered the craft.

Emma started the engine and it made a loud whining noise. Anesthesia hopped behind Ernst on his motorcycle and they both shot away. Emma and George could hear the sirens of the military police jeeps coming. The engine was not warmed up enough to elevate but she tried anyway. It was a bouncing lift but the craft did rise. It was slow but it got faster as the seconds ticked by. Finally the temperature was right and the flying saucer swished away.

Chapter 35

"Were are we going?" George asked when Emma leveled out. "Antarctica" Emma answered. "Why" he asked. "That's where the Angel said to go" she answered. "Did he tell you what we're doing when we get there?" he asked. Emma went silent. "Emma, I asked you a question" George said. "George we're going to do battle! That's all I know!" she answered and it really upset her. "God will be with us" George said. Emma flew the craft below the clouds to watch the sun come up in the East. It was a perfect day to see such an amazing sight flying over Central America. Emma put the craft on automatic pilot and went to the port hole to witness the sight, George followed her. "It's so sad that such a beautiful place has people in it that are so poor" Emma said. George didn't respond he just looked at the earth beneath them.

"Show me how to fire this weapon" he said. They both climbed up to the bubble on he top. They could see every where except what was directly underneath their flying machine. "This weapon doesn't fire bullets, it fires a light ray that can burn through metal like a knife through butter" Emma said. She pulled the trigger and a beam of red light shot into the sky. "It works like any other gun, just point and shoot" she said. George fired once to see how it worked.

"It's amazing how much technology the Nazis have" George said. "Believe me, they have plenty of help" Emma said. "What! Who on earth would help the Nazis?" George said. "No one" Emma answered. "Emma, you're talking in riddles" George said. "George, their help doesn't come from this earth" she said. "Oh, I guess you're going to say it comes from outer space" George teased. Emma gave George a very cold look and his smile went away. "That's where it comes from" she said seriously. George was perplexed. What Emma was saying was so wild but here he was fly in an aircraft that was so far advanced than any other flying machine on the face of the Earth.

"How do they get this information?" George asked. "The inhabitants of the planet Aldebaran contacted my Aunt Maria through a séance. She writes the instructions in an ancient language and some scholar interprets the message. "Emma, your Aunt is not getting her information from another planet. Those instruction are coming from one of Satan's angels" George said. "George, I have been at a séance with my Aunt and it was such an eerie thing" she told George. "In the séance, I blacked out and floated through space to that far away planet. The inhabitants lifted me to their shoulders and carried me to be sacrificed to a giant bull" she said. "The devil gave you a vision, it wasn't real" George told her. "But it seemed so real" she said. "Did you leave the room and come back?" he asked. "Then it wasn't real" he explained.

"How about this saucer? How do you explain this?" she asked, putting her hands out around turning in circles. "When Moses went before the Pharaoh he threw his rod to the floor and it turned into a snake. Then the Pharaoh's magicians did the same with their rods and they turned into snakes. The devil knows how to do stuff like that and he gave your Aunt the instructions" he said. "You've given me a lot to think about, George" she said. "Pray about it, Emma" he told her. She went back to the controls of the aircraft. Suddenly something flew straight at the saucer, it missed crashing into them by just a few feet. Then a voice came on the radio "Good to meet you again Emma Orsic are you ready to die?" it was the voice of Otto. "Man the weapon, George!" Emma yelled. George went right to it. "You might be surprised at who dies today, Otto" she said into the microphone.

Both flying machines did a U-turns and came at each other firing. They both were able to dodge each others laser beams. The dog fight went on and on. Emma and Otto were at equal skill flying the two saucers. They did barrel rolls and loop-the-loops. One moment she was chasing him and the next moment he was chasing her. Otto flew directly underneath Emma craft and struck the engine with the ray. Just as the light beam hit, Emma turned the craft upward in a 90 degree angle, George fired on Otto's craft a split second after he struck theirs.

Otto's craft was blown up into a million pieces. Smoke came from the bottom of the saucer and it started to descend. Emma tried everything she knew but nothing helped. Their flying machine struck down in the water and began to sink. And it took just a few seconds for it to land on the bottom of the ocean. The craft was water-tight, no water was coming in. Emma and George was trapped inside

Chapter 36

"We're possibly only ten or fifteen feet under water" George said. "But how far are we from land?" Emma remarked. "The water is very cold also" George returned. Emma looked down at the deck, she didn't want to say any more. "Well, we can't stay trapped in here, we have to do something" he said. Emma gave him a sad look. "I have a plan, I'll open up the hatch and the compartment will fill up with water. When it is filled completely up, we'll hold our breathe and swim to the surface" he suggested. "Like you said the water is very cold, besides, how long can you tread water?" she lamented. "Let's just try this, Emma" George said.

George took the wheel to the scuttle and turned it counter clockwise till it stopped. He tried to lift it open but it wouldn't budge. "Too much water pressure. I can't open it. Help me Emma" he said. Emma came to him but between the two of them them could not open the scuttle. Emma gave up and burst into tears. She sat on the deck and her body lost all of it's energy. "I'm so sorry, George I dragged you in this mess" she cried. "You did no such thing. I volunteered for this" he remarked.

George took a seat next to Emma on the deck and he put his arm around her. "We didn't know what that Nazi was up to. He could have done plenty of damage if he was headed to America" George said. "You're saying we accomplished something?" she asked George. "Yes Emma, this was all for a reason" he said. "But no one will ever know" she said. "God will know. The Angel knew" he said. They sat silently for a moment and watched fish swimming outside the port hole.

"George, I'm afraid" Emma said. George couldn't say a word. Then he spoke "Emma, I guess it doesn't matter now...I have been crazy in love with you since I first saw you" Emma stopped crying. "I really didn't want to smoke marijuana but I did it just to be near you" he admitted and looked away from her. Emma giggled. "That's how I thought you would react, Emma, but I wanted you to know how I feel about you" he said sadly. "George! George! No! When I first met you and you got high, you told the greatest stories about your home town. Madison Indiana, right?" she stated. "Ya, that's my home town" he said "George I loved your stories and some of them were so funny...I really liked you" she said. "But I looked like a fat little college professor..." he tried to say but. Emma interrupted him, "That day in Albuquerque, when you removed your crash helmet, I thought I was looking at the man of my dreams. Then I noticed it was you. I couldn't believe my eyes. George I thought I was going crazy" she went on and on. "Here I just ran into my brother who I haven't seen in years. Then I see you...who had undertaken a metamorphosis" she said. "All of it just just too much"

George was shocked, he sat silently on the deck of the flying saucer listening to the girl he had been in love with for years. "When we went into the store shopping for boots. Ernst hooked up with Anesthesia and we walked together...I wanted you to hold my hand so badly, George" she admitted. George shook his head in disbelief "It made me feel so good walking with you that day. I wanted the world to think you was my girl friend but I thought you would never feel that way about me." he said.

"George, it's funny but I'm no longer afraid to die" Emma said. "I feel the same way Emma" he return. They looked into each others eyes, George brush her cheek with his fingers. "George lets Make...." George interrupted her before she got it out. "No! We're not married!" he said. "Would you marry me if you could?" she asked. "In a heartbeat" he answered. "Then George it's okay" she said. "We're not married and we're about to die. Do you want to take that chance?" he said. "God knows we love one another.....Who married Adam and Eve?" she said. "Emma, I think I hear something" George said. "C'mon George don't change the subject" Emma said. "No I really do hear something" he repeated. They both stopped talking then Emma heard it. "It's a ship" George said. "It may not hear us us on the sonar, make some noise" Emma shouted. They both hammered away on the hull with whatever they could put in their hands.

The humming got louder and louder and Emma and George was near to being suffocated. Sudden the humming stopped and it sounded like it was right above them. Emma passed out but George saw a scuba driver through the port hole and he waved and he yelled "hurry!" and the diver read his lips. He quickly looked through the port hole and saw Emma lying on the deck. The diver put hooks fastened to some cables through the pad-eyes on the flying saucer. Then he swam to the surface and in a few seconds the craft was being raised from the bottom of the ocean. The diver came back and grabbed the outside wheel of the scuttle. As soon as the craft broke the surface, the diver turned the wheel to open the compartment. When he opened it George was lifting Emma up to the Diver. He lifted her out and laid her flat on the hull of the craft. George climbed out and laid down beside her. The diver gave Emma mouth to mouth. Emma came to and sat up. All the sailors watching from the ship cheered.

Chapter 37

"Thank God you showed up when you did!" George said while his senses were returning to him. "Your name is George Matthews and she is Emma Orsic, am I right?" he asked. "Yes. Are we under arrest?" he asked. "I can't say for sure but what I can say is, I'm very glad you blasted that Foo-fighter out of the sky. There is no way of knowing what kind of damage he could have done in the United States" the CPO told him. "Did you see us?" George asked. "We saw the entire dogfight, You two are Cracker-Jacks" he told them. "I've never shot anything bigger than a squirrel" he told the Chief. "I'm going to have to go hunting with you" he remarked. Soon they discovered Admiral Byrd's flotilla rescued them.

The flying saucer was brought on board the USS Canisteo (AO-99) and George and Emma was taken to sick-bay immediately. The ship's doctor examined them and they were in perfect health. The ship's captain wanted to honor the two hero's with an elegant diner in the ward-room. Everyone was to dress formal. For the officers, they were to wear their Dress-blues but that presented a problem for the two civilians. A Lieutenant J.G. loaned George the second set of Dress-blues that he had and they fit him well. There was no women on the ship and Emma was dressed in Olive-drab coveralls. She felt embarrassed but the lieutenant came through again. He was engaged to be married to a girl back home. He bought her a wedding dress when his ship stopped in France. He rolled the dress up Navy tight and stowed it in his locker. He presented it to Emma saying "If you wear this without the head covering, no one will know it's a wedding dress"

Emma's heart melted when she entered the Ward-room in the satin white dress. The Navy officers jumped to Attention as she walked in. The Captain left his seat at the front of the room and walked to her, he took her arm and escorted her to his table. There she sat between him and George dressed in Navy dress-blues. She couldn't stop blushing. The Stewards prepared a steak and lobster diner better than any chef in Paris could have. After the meal the Captain gave a speech about George and Emma's bravery and it was finished with a huge applause. Then the officers sang "Anchors aweigh" and followed it by sing "God bless America" What an evening it was for George and Emma.

Chapter 38

Two days later, a PMB-5 Mariner, seaplane was launched from the USS Pine Island (AV-12) and Emma was on board the plane. The brave soul insisted on going with the pilots because she could recognize the hidden base from the air "I know what I'm looking for" she insisted. The Captain kept saying "No" to her so she went over his head and asked Admiral Byrd if she could go on the aerial survey of Antarctica. The Admiral granted her permission to go.

She told everyone concerned that when she escaped the hidden base, her and Otto flew in a straight path to New Mexico. "We did not waver one square inch from fling a direct straight line northward. We didn't fly over any land as we left Antarctica" she told them. "There's another clue to the base, sometimes a U-boat is moored outside the entrance but they don't stay there very long" she said. The Captain then realized it was a great idea for her to go on the mission.

The seaplane Emma flew in was nicknamed the "Lucky Duck." The plane was very clean and *squared away*. There was a place for everything needed and the crew of seven knew every item onboard the craft. They knew what it's function was and where it was stored. The only things that were extras were the photographs of the crews wives and girlfriends. Flying above the Antarctic was not comfortable. The August temperature was only 23 degrees Fahrenheit and flying at the speed of 100mph made it very cold inside the plane. Emma was bundle up like an Eskimo and she couldn't stop shivering. She sat directly behind the two pilots and had a great view of the earth beneath them.

Emma had the Pilots fly lower because something looked familiar to her. The closer they flew the more familiar that area looked. They flew in a wide circle around the area before they lowered to an unsafe height.

Emma spotted the cave she was looking for so the plane flew by only a few feet off the surface of the water. They all looked inside the cave. "There's no doors! There should be double doors just inside the opening. How did they hide them!" Emma yelled. "It's not the right cave, Miss Orsic. It may look like the right one but it isn't" the pilot told her. "It looks so much like the right one" she said in anger. "Don't fret it, we get tricked all the time in this business" the Pilot encouraged her.

"I see something flying at eleven o'clock" one of the crew said over the sound power microphone/headset. The Pilot grabbed his binoculars and look in the 11: 00 o'clock direction. "Theirs another plane in the sky" he announced to the crew. "Gunners man your positions" he ordered over the microphone. "Radio, notify the Pine Island and let them know we have spotted another plane" The Pilot ordered the radioman. The other plane began to fly toward them. The pilot looked through the binoculars again. "It's a Nazi Heinkel HE 115 Seaplane" The Pilot announced. Emma noticed the crew became worried by the Pilot's announcement "What's the Problem?" she asked the Copilot. "That plane can maneuver much better than we can" the Copilot answered.

The two planes flew directly toward one another, when they crossed paths, they were only a few feet from crashing in to each other. The maneuver was a challenge of bravery. Within a minute the Nazi plane did a U turn and slowly flew next to the "Lucky Duck." The two enemy pilots gave each other a dirty looks, Then he fired his fixed nose gun. The pilot gave the Nazi an angry look. "Nose gunner, fire into the air" the Pilot ordered. And the Nose Gunner shot a few rounds. "This could get ugly. He might be more agile but we have a tail gunner and a nose gunner compared to his Nose Gunner only" the Pilot told Emma. "You should go below, Miss Orsic" he told her and she obeyed.

The Nazi plane pulled away at full throttle and the "Lucky Duck" followed. The Enemy plane was much faster but once he around a mile away he slowed so the American could catch him. The Heinkel turned it's nose up and began to climb and it made the PMB-5 look clumsy. The cat and mouse game continued for a half hour till the enemy Seaplane began to descend. It kept flying downward and finally it landed in the ocean. The lucky Duck flew by leaving it alone.

"I saw something in the water, earlier. Turn around, quickly!" Emma yelled into the sound powered microphone. Everyone was surprised because they were watching the enemy aircraft and not the sea below them. "I think I saw a U boat! fly downward! fly downward!" She yelled again. The Pilot practically put the seaplane in a nose dive. "I see it in the water at 2:00 o'clock!" one of the crew announced and the pilot flew down in that direction. A few seconds later they saw the Conning tower of a German U boat sink under the water.

"I saw something else. Go to 9:00 o'clock and fly straight" Emma said. The pilot leveled off and went to 9:00 O'clock. "What did you see, Miss Orsic?" The Pilot asked. "I saw the base, I'm sure this time!" she answered. Thirty seconds later they saw another U boat leaving it's hidden port and directly behind it was was the double door of the secret base. The entire crew saw it and began to cheer. "It looks like they're run...we're just one plane" the Co-pilot said. "We have the Atom Bomb" the pilot said.

The Pilot flew around the area twice, taking plenty of photos as they went. Then the hidden door of the roof opened and two flying saucers three times bigger than the one Emma flew ascended out. They both climb to around one thousand feet then dart away at an unbelievable speed. They were out of sight in five second. The crew aboard the lucky duck was stunned. They flew back to the enemy Seaplane and saw the crew of three entering one of the U boats they flew in circles watch what was happening until the submarine pulled away and dived under the water.

Book two of the Orsic Papers trilogy. Maria Orsic stalks the baby-boomer son of George and Emma Matthews, named Jim. Her purpose is t to reclaim the very last world war two Nazi flying saucer

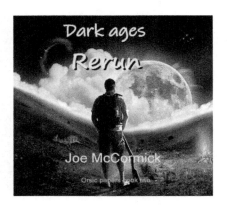

Book trree of the Orsic Papers trilogy. "The War about Forever." Set in the year 2053, the world has fallen back into the Dark Ages due to bad political policies. Only a small portion of the Unites States remain free. Wilbur Matthews and his father secretly construct a craft that can act as a plane, a boat, a submarine, and an automobile. Wilbur and his twin sister, Wilma, were separated when they were infants. Wilbur steals the craft (Airphib) and finds his sister. They along with their friends help reunite the USA

Made in the USA
Middletown, DE
02 April 2023

28076061R00050